The
HUNT
for the
HOLY GRAIL

written by

PRESTON WILLIAM CHILD
& MATTHEW KING

D1527959

Heiken Marketing

Heiken Marketing
heikenmarketing@gmail.com

Publisher's Note: This is a work of fiction. Names, characters, places, and incidents are a product of the author's imagination. Locales and public names are sometimes used for atmospheric purposes. Any resemblance to actual people, living or dead, or to businesses, companies, events, institutions, or locales is completely coincidental.

Edited (USA) by Anna Drago

CHAPTER 1:

In the Pentagon there was a small room. It was the size of a closet, and rudely furnished. Most employees of the most famous government building did not even know that it existed. Even the bordering conference rooms and offices were populated with government agents who had only a vague idea of what happened in the room in question.

"It's some kind of Geography – or Geology thing. I don't know," is what Secretary of State Harris said the President when they walked by on the way to a conference room some years before.

The people who made their way in and out of the room did not go out of the way to make themselves conspicuous either. They looked as if they were visitors to the building, on a tour or just passing through. They do not dress in the standard issue white shirt, black suit, black tie of other Pentagon employees. They were typically wearing dark corduroys, wrinkled plaid shirts with coffee and dirt stains on the cuffs, and hair as equally messy. They were not geologists and geographers, but archaeologists, and they were part of an underappreciated task force within the Department of Defense. They were called the Relevant Relic Recovery Committee – typical government speak which translated in practical terms to the recovery of ancient items that could lead to diplomatic or economic victories. Their activities were usually limited to finding items that made the United States government look good.

But there was one frequenter of the closet-sized room who worked on something entirely different. He spent his time looking for something that had no bearing on present events as the Pentagon would have seen it. He saw things a bit differently. His name was Mark Lockheed, and he was looking for the Holy Grail.

He opened the door to what its inhabitants lovingly called "the Hole" and the door, as it always did, brushed up against the conference room table that (although sawed in half) did not fit in the tiny room. It was approximately the size of a ten year old boy's bedroom, and about as tidy as one too. There was a conference table, a small sink, and a chalkboard. The chalkboard was covered with months old fliers for museum exhibits. The ceiling was oppressively low and the lighting was harsh and clinical.

"Guys, the minister is here!" The shouter was Tom Gates, a man who fit more into the mold of what the Pentagon wanted the inhabitants of the hole to be. He did his due diligence, finding trinkets to give as gifts to ayatollahs and rabbis to smooth over conflicts, and he kept his head down. "The Minister" was his nickname for Mark. He and some other members of the committee thought that they did not receive more respect from the higher-ups because people like Mark made them look like crackpots searching for things that never existed in the first place.

"Great to see you too, Gates. Heard you're headed to Egypt. Shouldn't you go ahead and leave? Can't be too early to the airport these days am I right?"

"How would you know, Lockheed? You haven't been out of this room in five years. Some of us look for things, not childhood fantasies."

Mark ignored the jibe and headed straight for the coffeemaker. It was already going to be a long day without getting into an argument with Tom. His friend and sympathizer, Kathy Rollins was at the coffeemaker already, pouring grounds into the filter.

"Ignore him," she said.

"You don't have to tell me twice. You on assignment too I hear?"

"Ship out to Beirut next week."

Mark smiled at Kathy. He had always had a crush on her, but as most men who end up as Biblical archaeologists he was not a ladies' man. He suspected that she knew about his feelings. She was the only one in the department who ever encouraged him about his project.

"What have you got going on today?" she asked.

Mark told her about his meeting, which was essentially an audit. Members of the committee had to meet with management on a supposedly random basis to explain their costs and usefulness to the government as an archaeologist. Mark was not looking forward to the meeting, despite the fact that he cost the government only his pitiful salary. He did not collect any premiums. The members of the committee received a premium, in addition to their base salary, every time they brought a useful artifact in. As a result of his grail obsession, for years Mark had only been pulling in his salary, and his decrepit box of an apartment showed it.

"Harsh," she said. "But drinks to celebrate if you survive?"

Kathy invited Mark to get drinks about once a week, and he generally declined. He went every once in a while, out of fear of losing his one ally in the office. It was always an awkward affair at a DC bar that was frequented by mostly politicians. It was not an environment that Mark felt he fits into.

"Yeah," he said. "Let's do that. I pick the place this time."

"You got a deal."

Mark stirred some powdered creamer into his coffee with a plastic spoon and saw Tom Gates flip him the bird. His dirt encrusted middle fingernail reflected the powerful fluorescent overhead light of the hole.

CHAPTER 2:

Mark walked along 10th street, thinking about his meeting and killing time before meeting Kathy. He had not lost his job, but they had very firmly insisted that he make his main project more of a hobby, and less of a project that government dollars were spent on. He had been instructed to come up with a proposal within two weeks for a potentially useful gig: even if it was only a "good press" gig. A good press gig usually involved the attempt to find dinosaur bones or some other nonsense that Mark had no interest in. A good press gig did not even have to get results or find anything other than dirt. Management just liked putting out a press release about how the government was making great progress in looking for newly undiscovered traces of dinosaurs. The tour guides at the Smithsonian had to have something to talk about.

Mark kicked a can in front of him as he walked. He did not want to fruitlessly dig for dinosaur bones. He wanted to find the Holy Grail. It has been his passion for his entire life. He had irritated his father to no end about it. Mark's father, before his death, had been a minister, and he was always concerned about Mark's interest in the scriptures. Mark's interest was nearly always centered not on the gospel, but on more practical matters. One of his very first Biblical questions for his father had been about the grail.

"But what happened to the cup?" little Mark asked his father as he sat on the edge of his race car bed.

"What cup?"

"You know, the one. When he had given thanks he said drink from it all of you."

"How should I know, Mark? What's important to remember about the book of Matthew—"

"But it was a real cup right? It's not one of those things that are just a metaphor? Because you can't drink out of a metaphorical cup. Then it could still be out there somewhere, under the ground, or even in someone's house!"

His father sighed and kissed his son on the forehead. He closed his Bible and told his son that it was lights out in fifteen minutes.

He thought about his father and how they became closer as the old man had neared death. Mark was never going to be able to look at the Bible as his father did, despite his nickname. But he could not help but feel that his quest was partially for his father. If there was anything his father would feel worthy of finding, it would be something held by Jesus. His father's life was a love affair with the long gone Savior, and while Mark could not reconcile his scientific training with his father's religion; he felt this was a suitable way to honor the man. He could not help but think his father would be proud of him for finding the cup of Christ.

Mark checked his watch and saw that it was nearly eight. He took a right and picked up his pace. He was going to be late if he did not hurry. Something cold and hard hit Mark on the head and his world went black. He could vaguely feel the concrete come up to meet his face and then there was nothing. He woke up with Kathy shaking him and ripping off the bottom of her blouse. She was using it to staunch the bleeding from his nose and another piece to wipe the blood from his eyes. As far as he could tell, he was still in the same spot where he had checked his watch.

"Kathy?"

"Hey there, old buddy. You didn't quite make it to the bar. When I got worried I walked around the block and here you were."

"Here I am. Not my best day."

"No, I'd imagine not."

"You know—I'm not a menacing guy. I'd probably have given him my wallet. I think it had seven bucks in it. I guess drinks are on you."

He sat up and attempted to stand. He wobbled.

"I think the emergency room is a better idea than drinks," she said.

"Screw that noise."

He managed to stand up this time and feel the back of his head. There was a big bump and he almost certainly had a big gash on his forehead from hitting the pavement. His nose was miraculously intact.

"Okay. One drink. Then you are at least going home to take it easy. Maybe take tomorrow off."

"Archaeologists never say die," he said and they both laughed. Kathy supported him on her shoulder and they made their way to the bar.

After a few drinks, Kathy insisted on walking him home "to prove that chivalry is not dead" and Mark accepted. She took his apartment key from him and opened the door. She held it open as Mark flopped down on his couch. Normally, he would have cared about Kathy seeing his tiny apartment, but he did not care after the day he had had.

"Nice place," she said.

"No need to lie, Kathy. Want the tour?" He waved his arms in a circle around his head. "And you've had it."

"It's well kept," she said. "Are you sure you're going to be alright?"

He gave her a big thumbs up. She adjusted her purse on her shoulder and leaned down over Mark. Their breath mingled for the fraction of a second before she put her lips on his.

"I had fun," she said.

"Me too. Now."

"Do call if you need anything."

She closed his apartment door behind her and Mark fell back and into a blissful sleep almost immediately.

He was most rudely interrupted.

CHAPTER 3:

Mark was rudely interrupted from his pleasant dreams by an unbearably loud pounding on his apartment door. He cursed under his breath and got up. He wrapped a blanket around himself and looked through his peephole. It was simply black. His brain was still wreathed in sleep and he did not think further than it was probably very dark outside. His sleepy brain did not consider that someone could be holding their gloved hand over the hole. He opened the door and a hood immediately went over his head. He nearly laughed to himself. The last twelve hours of his life had been utterly preposterous. He allowed his body to relax as the men picked him up and carried him to what he imagined (quite correctly) was the back of a van. At least, he thought, this put his meeting with the suits in perspective. He did not know how long they drove for, but he imagined, as he saw as many spy movies as the next guy, that they might be simply driving him in circles. He was strangely calm and not scared. They had not harmed him and they even put a seatbelt on him. He rode calmly and waited for whatever was coming.

Finally, the ride came to an end and he could feel a rough gloved hand reach across him to undo his seatbelt. A gravelly voice said,

"Wouldn't want our prize archaeologist to get hurt now would we?"

They marched him across wet grass and into a place where their footsteps echoed. Here, they finally took the hood off and he could see that there were only two men with him, and he was in a warehouse of sorts, surrounded by fancy cars. He saw Lamborghinis, Ferraris, Porsches, and Bentleys, both old and new. He thought he saw a Model-T in the far corner but he did not have time to figure it out. One of the men, a gray-bearded, intimidating man who Mark imagined was his seatbelt man, grabbed him by the shoulder and led him towards the door.

"He's waiting," he said.

9

Mark was lead up a staircase and into an elaborate kitchen. Before he had time to be awed by the kitchen, he was directed into a living room, where an old man sat in front of a fire. There was a Doberman that sat at attention on his right, and the man absentmindedly stroked the dog's head. The man's feet were up on an ottoman. He wore house slippers and his legs were casually crossed at the ankle. He was clean-shaven; his face reflected the flickering light of the fire. He was dressed as for a dinner party, in a tuxedo and bowtie, and his hair was neatly parted on the right side. His hair was all white, but he carried it off with the confidence of a man who had come to terms with aging.

"Welcome," he said to Mark. "Please sit down Mr. Lockheed. I'm very sorry for the er—manner of our meeting, if you will. It was a necessary precaution as you will find out."

Mark took the seat indicated to him, which was a tall-backed and comfortable armchair, stylishly diagonal to the fire and the old man.

"My name is Reginald Astair, and I believe you can help me."

"I'm not typically in the business of helping those who mug me."

"Mug?" The old man looked alarmed and shot daggers with his eyes at the men who brought Mark in. "Did you treat this man roughly? Mr. Lockheed, I can assure you that they were given the strictest instructions with how to deal with you. They were supposed to treat you with the utmost—"

"No, I meant earlier today."

"Earlier?"

"You didn't have me mugged?"

"Why in God's name would I do that? Of course not."

"Well you must understand with the situation that I'm in it doesn't seem too far-fetched."

"Point taken, Mr. Lockheed. Let me see if I can adequately explain why I have brought you here. I do sincerely commiserate you for your bad luck with earlier, but that is our fair city is it not? Do you need medical attention? – I could make sure you're well taken care off."

Mark shook his head no. He was curious and wanted to hear what the old man had to say.

"As I said, I believe you can help me. We have a similar fascination in this life, Mr. Lockheed. I think you probably know what that is."

Mark kept his poker face.

"The Holy Grail. It has been my fascination as well as yours, and I have something that your current position could not offer you: support, money, belief. In so many words, Mr. Lockheed. I want you to find me the grail."

"How do you know I'm looking for it?"

"I can't tell you that, I'm afraid."

"Why was I kidnapped?"

"I thought we'd get to that. There are some people in this city, though you may find it hard to believe, given your experiences, who take the finding of the grail very seriously. I am by no means the only one with their eyes on you. I am—or rather I think I am the most honest of the lot, though that does not qualify me for a Nobel. And I happened to hear...through various sources of information, that another, less scrupulous seeker of the grail planned to do this very thing to you on your way to work in the morning. I can assure you that he would not have been so accommodating."

The old man smiled a toothy smile at Mark and showed a gold tooth.

"Well you're right about one thing."

"And that is?"

"It is hard to believe. In fact, I was told just this morning that I have to abandon it for all intents and purposes."

"Perfect timing," the old man said.

"Mr. Astair," Mark said. "What exactly are you offering?"

"Any amount of money you wish. It is not an issue. You will also receive whatever support you need, travel arrangements, etc. I believe that you can do it. I've paid close attention to your career."

"How close?"

"I've read your paper on the flight of Judas."

"It's just academic theorizing. Nonsense really."

"I don't think you believe that Mr. Lockheed."

11

Mark looked the old man up and down and what he saw was a tremendous eagerness. This man had truly been waiting to see him. He even looked somewhat starstruck. He was the opposite of everyone at the Pentagon. He believed that Mark was an important figure and useful to his profession. Mark saw a man who shared his passion. He, strangely, was able to look past the kidnapping. He found the man's explanation to be satisfactory, if a bit vague. He folded his fingers together and looked at Reginald Astair.

"I have a few conditions."

CHAPTER 4:

Mark stood nervously in the hangar, bouncing up and down on his heels. Astair said he could have whoever he wanted as a team, and he wanted Kathy. Just yesterday morning he would not have cared, but not even the thought of a fully-funded grail project could shake the image burned into his brain of Kathy closing her eyes and leaning over him to kiss him. She was his choice.

He saw her approach just as the Cessna Citation Longitude behind him kicked into gear and the sound was deafening. Her dress was blowing up around her knees and she held it down with her palms, doing her best Marilyn Monroe impression. She screamed something at him but he could not hear. He gestured inside the plane and she looked skeptical. He mouthed trust me and they both climbed the stairs and up into the passenger compartment. Reginald Astair was already aboard, sipping a gin and tonic. His Doberman, who, as Mark had learned on the previous day, was named Lucifer, sat upright next to him.

"Kathy Rollins, Reginald Astair," Mark said. Reginald Astair stood and offered his hand to the young woman.

"A pleasure, my dear."

Kathy wore a look of supreme confusion, but Mark assured her he could explain everything. She insisted that she had to get to work but Mark asked her if she could please sit down. The plane took off moments later.

"Where are we going?" she said.

"Think of it as a date," Mark responded, the last few hours of his life giving him greater confidence than he had ever had before.

"Oh really? A date, in a plane, with this fellow and his dog? We have different ideas of romance, though your acknowledgement of my eligibility after all these years is appreciated."

Reginald Astair laughed heartily.

"I like this girl," he said. "She has the right attitude."

Mark still smiled. He knew that once he explained what they were up to, she would be excited. She was, after all, an archaeologist.

"I think you had better do some explaining," Reginald said.

"Mr. Astair here has agreed to generously fund my search for the grail. We are currently headed to Paris to speak to my college professor, Dr. LeTrec."

"And assuming I approve of you sweeping me away to Paris on a job that I didn't ask to be a part of...which mind you, is a big assumption, what part does Dr. LeTrec play in this?"

"He was my professor when I wrote an article that is of particular interest to grail-hunters, including Mr. Astair. Dr. LeTrec helped me write it. It's called 'The Final Flight of Judas' and it was not widely published. I was something of a laughingstock among the intellectual community."

"What's it about?"

"Are you sure you want to hear?"

"Well you essentially kidnapped me."

"You know...I know the feeling," he said.

Kathy and Reginald Astair (though he was already very familiar with the text) listened raptly as Mark detailed his article that he wrote more than ten years ago. The article sought to refute the Biblical idea that Judas hung himself from a tree from the shame of his betrayal of Christ. Mark's portrayal of Judas was more in line with how people tend to behave psychologically. Mark posited in his article that Judas was much more likely to have been a ruthless opportunist, as he sold out Christ. The idea of him killing himself after the fact was not psychologically consistent. There was an ancient document that Mark spoke of, that was mentioned in some obscure Greek texts that had been uncovered, that allegedly described the flight of Judas from Jerusalem across the Mediterranean and into Cyprus. The text also described Judas as a petty thief and opportunist who did not leave Jerusalem without a purloined lot of goodies taken from the one whom he had betrayed, including the Holy Grail, which he was said to have sold for very little shortly thereafter in order to buy ale. This text was said to have originally been discovered in 1668. The Catholic Church, led by Pope Clement IX at this point, sought to destroy the document, as they seek to destroy anything that directly contradicts the word of God. There was considerable controversy about whether or not the document existed at all, or if it had actually been destroyed, but its whereabouts were unknown if it still existed. Mark speculated that this theory was in line with everything historically known about the Catholic Church and that there was a statistically significant possibility that it did exist and that the grail, if it still existed, was on the island of Cyprus.

"Whoa," Kathy said.

"An apt description," said Reginald Astair. "Would you like to know the fee your friend has arranged should you choose to accept? You are of course welcome to enjoy your free trip to Paris and return home later today at my expense, should you so choose."

"That won't be necessary. I'm absolutely in," she said, looking at Mark with a passion in her eyes that he had never seen in a woman before. "But what about our jobs at the Pentagon?"

Mark reached underneath his seat and pulled out a manila folder.

"We don't have any other jobs," he said calmly. He handed Kathy the folder.

"What is this?" she said.
"Our new identities."

CHAPTER 5:

There was no denying the glamor of Paris. Archaeologists were used to travel, but their destinations were usually more of a sandy variety, and not the easygoing old-world metropolis also known as the city of love. Reginald Astair looked at home wading through the tufts of people on the street, as if he was born into it. Kathy and Mark walked behind him, taking in the smells of the city. They walked by a Jewish bakery and the sweet smell of challah had their mouths watering. Even the cigarette smoke seemed to be more pleasant, though Mark almost collided with some passers-by following his nose as he walked. He had never felt so anonymous, but so powerful at the same time. He was unknown among the streets. None of these Frenchmen and women who passed carelessly by, knew that he and the woman whose arm was linked with his, and the eccentric and mysteriously wealthy man in front of them, were on the greatest quest that man could aspire to. It was thrilling and terrifying. Kathy squeezed his hand as if she knew what he was thinking.

They were heading towards a dingy office building on Rue Bonaparte, just across the Seine from the Louvre, where Dr. LeTrec had his office. He was no longer a professor of archaeology, but a retailer of "fine art" as he termed it, or more accurately: a seller of cheap knockoffs to tourists. His career as a professor had been cut short by his penchant for wine that went well beyond French normal, and into the territory of alcoholism. He explained this to them as they sat in his office, though Reginald Astair was already aware of the fact, as his men prepared a dossier for him on Dr. LeTrec that he had read on the plane.

"Ms. Copperfield, my cousin," was how Mark introduced Kathy to his old professor. Obviously, Dr. LeTrec knew who Mark was, so he could not try out his new identity, but LeTrec absentmindedly signed the non-disclosure agreement that Reginald slid across his desk when they arrived.

"So what's this all about anyway? Bringing your cousin and your lawyer across the deep blue just to see an old teacher? I know you aren't here to buy a Titian copy done by a wino off the Château Rouge metro stop."

"No. We are not here for that," Mark said. "But in a way...we are here to talk about old times."

They left Dr. LeTrec to think about what they had told him. They made plans to meet him back at his office the next day when he assured them he would have an answer.

* * *

"He'll do it," Reginald said confidently. "It's better than selling hack artwork. He's playing at negotiating because he's wily. But he'll do it."

"I think he's right," Kathy said, picking up a blouse and holding it up to her figure. "What do you think, Mark?"

They were in the process of buying Kathy a new wardrobe, as she was brought along on the trip without the knowledge that she would be going on a trip at all.

"Lovely, my dear," Reginald said before Mark had a chance to comment. Mark smiled at her and nodded his agreement. It was a fetching blouse.

* * *

It was the blouse she was wearing the next morning at eleven a.m. sharp (Dr. LeTrec not being an early riser) when they arrived again at the stairs to his office. They rang the buzzer a dozen times and there was no response. They were all worried, and it was a full hour after their arrival before a groggy groan was heard over the speaker as the button was pushed and the door opened. They found Dr. LeTrec in his bathrobe, not entirely closed, dropping Alka-Seltzer tablets into a glass of water. He motioned for them to sit down across from him. Reginald Astair was not pleased. He glared at the Frenchman.

"Have you come to a decision?" the rich old man demanded impatiently with the voice of a man who was used to getting what he wanted. It occurred to Mark for the most fleeting of moments, that up until this point, Reginald Astair had gotten everything that he wanted.

"Is there any way," Dr. LeTrec said, "you could speak less loudly?"

Reginald Astair stood up and grabbed Dr. LeTrec by his robe. He pulled him up so that they were face to face.

"At one point in your pathetic life, you were a genius. I know that, because I have read your essays and been in awe of you. But I am not in awe of this," he paused for effect. "riffraff...before me. You disgust me, and if it were not for your old friend here I don't think I would even include you in this incredible opportunity. Now tell me, have you come to a decision?"

He had come to a decision.

In their hotel room that night, after discussing the next day's journey, Kathy and Mark discussed Reginald being frightening at that moment. They had not seen that side of the old man before.

They thought that they were speaking privately, but it so occurred that they were not.

CHAPTER 6:

Their globetrotting continued the next morning. They were not headed for Cyprus yet, but first for Jerusalem. Any true search for the Holy Grail must first begin in Jerusalem. There was no discussion about this. They were all versed enough in grail lore to know this.

Mark tried to ignore the bloodshot eyes and broken facial capillaries of his old professor as they headed back to the Cessna. He put his hand on his teacher's shoulder.

"I really think we're going to find it," Mark said.

"It would be incredible," Dr. LeTrec answered, but his heart was not in it. "Really incredible, Mark." He patted Mark on the back and they both walked up the steps to the plane and into the most dangerous journey of their lives. It was a long flight and they had to make a stopover for refueling in Istanbul. After the second takeoff Mark got up and went to the bathroom. Reginald was reading something from a folder, and Dr. LeTrec was snoring loudly.

Mark did not bother to lock the bathroom door and immediately after he closed it, it opened again and Kathy eased her way into the bathroom and closed the door behind her. She locked it.

"How does a plane this small have a bathroom this big?" she said, smiling fetchingly. Mark nearly shivered as he remembered the gleaming golden tooth of Reginald's smile. "Is that a couch?" she said. "In a fucking airplane bathroom. Wow."

"Yeah, it's something," Mark said. "Although I think technically that's a loveseat, not a couch."

"Even better," she said, edging towards Mark and forcing him to walk backwards towards the loveseat. He fell back into it and Kathy sat herself down on his lap.

Mark's thoughts that had been plaguing him as he walked to the bathroom, how Reginald had acted towards his old professor, and the absurd amount of money that he had put forward with no thought, among others, faded away as Kathy slowly unbuttoned her blouse and smirked at him as his own got caught on his watch.

"I'm an archaeologist," he said. "Not James Bond."

"We'll see about that…James," she whispered in his ear bevor reaching out and dimming the bathroom lights.

* * *

If either the professor or the mysterious old billionaire had any idea what had just happened, they did not let it show, but continued their conversation about the best cafes in Paris. The conversation felt strained. Mark involuntarily cleared his throat and Reginald shuffled some papers.

"Perhaps we should discuss our plans for tomorrow. The professor and I were discussing it when you two were er— indisposed, and we have some definite ideas." Reginald gave the Frenchman a nod and Dr. LeTrec began nervously.

"Right. Well, as you all undoubtedly know, tradition has it that Jesus walked the Via Dolorosa of the old city of Jerusalem as he bore the cross. Whether or not you believe he was divine, most people hold this to be true. We are going to perform a bit of a thought experiment. Really—if we are to engross ourselves at all in a search for the grail, we must admit from the beginning that it could end up being entirely a thought exercise."

Reginald winced at this, but the professor continued. "We'll walk the path of suffering and consider whether or not we think Judas would stick around to watch this. Mark had already stated in print that he believes Judas was long gone by this point, on a boat crossing the Mediterranean. This is, of course, what we base our trip on. And I must admit to still, after all these years, being taken by Mark's theory. Presumably, walking the path to the crucifixion will not change our minds, and we will proceed across the Mediterranean. We will, as Reginald and I have discussed, try and perform the journey as accurately as we can, going by Mark's paper as a guide. Are we of one mind?"

"I've got a question," Mark said. Kathy looked at him surprised, and saw that her hand was on his shoulder. She left it there.

"Yes, Mark?" Dr. LeTrec said.

"Are there any snacks on this plane? I'm starving.

CHAPTER 7:

Landing in Israel did not have the effect on Mark that landing in France had. While Paris lived up to its romantic nickname, Israel lived up to its well-known precarious position within the Middle East by the massive presence of military everywhere. Mark noticed as they went from Ben Gurion Airport to the hotel, after thoroughly checking by customs (Mark had been relieved that the passports provided by Reginald had passed inspection) that the people of the ancient city look tired, haggard. They did not look dejected, or sad, but simply worn down.

He was amazed by the ancient architecture, but equally amazed by the three burned out cars that they saw on their way. One of Reginald's men who met them at the airport was driving their vehicle while the other one was following them in another. They were meant to be protection, but Mark could not help but feel entrapped by them.

They were surly looking men with wraparound sunglasses and green cargo pants. On the way to the vehicles, they had waddled with the distinctive walk of men who were carrying concealed weapons.

Their hotel was more like a compound, and Jerusalem was more like a prison to Mark's eyes; a very beautiful, very old, and very sad prison. He tried to focus his mind on the task at hand, but found himself thinking of his father again. How had that man he so revered believed that the son of God had come from a place such as this? Mark wanted to find the grail, but he did not believe it would give him or anyone else eternal life. He knew that the power of the cup was in the myth that had surrounded it for so long. He did believe very strongly that when the minds of many people endow an object with power, in some sense, that power becomes a reality.

"Are you alright?" Kathy said. They were sharing a hotel room. Reginald said nothing, but gave only one key to Mark.

"Yeah. Just thinking about what we're doing."

"Don't want to do too much of that. You'll use up all your brainpower before we begin our thought experiments."

"It's not that. I believe what I wrote. I am certain, that if it exists, it's in Cyprus. I was just thinking about my dad...and some other things."

"Your dad?"

"He was a minister. He wouldn't see the point of this. But I want to find it for him anyway."

It made Mark think about Reginald's motives for finding the grail. Was he a religious man? He certainly did not particularly seem like one.

"And?"

"And what?"

"What else are you thinking about?"

"It's nothing. We should really clean up and get to bed. We've got a big day tomorrow. We're walking the path of suffering. There's just no way that can be fun."

"But you don't believe do you?"

"I believe that making someone carry a cross through town before you nail it to him is brutal and inhumane. And I believe that the trail of suffering is probably aptly named."

Mark was sitting on his bed and Kathy walked towards him. She hunched down and kissed his lips, before she turned around and walked to the bathroom, grabbing a towel from the hook as she went. Mark lay back on the bed and ran his hands through his hair. He was startled as he heard the bathroom door open. Kathy stuck her head out.

"Aren't you coming?" Steam leaked out of the crack in the door and rose to the ceiling. "I don't want the water to get cold."

"Of course," he grinned, getting up off the bed. "We certainly would not want that to happen."

CHAPTER 8:

The morning came quickly and mercilessly, and there was a knock on their hotel room door before the sun had risen. Mark got out of bed to find that it was the professor.

"May I?" he asked. Mark stepped aside and let his former teacher come into the room. Kathy looked up groggily and pulled the sheets up to her chin.

"Sorry to intrude," Dr. LeTrec said. "Just wanted to talk for a minute. Do you mind if we go into the bathroom?"

"Pardon?"

"Just follow me."

The professor walked into their bathroom and turned on not only the sink, but the shower. He closed the door and whispered to Mark.

"I found something in my room last night."

"Was it paranoia?"

"My room is bugged. I picked up the phone to dial the front desk for an extra towel, and when I accidentally dropped the receiver, there it was. I put my cellphone next to it and there was negative feedback. We're being listened to, and probably watched."

Mark let this soak in for a minute, and he had to admit to himself that the steam being created by the shower helped him to wake up and think more clearly.

"We've got Reginald's men protecting us," he said. "I'm sure we'll be fine."

"What if it's Reginald's men that are watching us?" LeTrec said.

Mark didn't want to admit his feelings about Reginald's men, or his fears he had about the operation as a whole, but it couldn't be crazy if the professor was feeling it too.

"Well maybe he's protecting his investment. He is paying us an awful lot of money. You aren't considering backing out, are you?"

"Well...no. I, er, need the money pretty badly. But I'm uncomfortable with it. I wanted to tell you. You'll keep Kathy in the loop?"

"I assume you mean Ms. Copperfield? Now more than ever, professor. We've got to stick to the identities."

"You're right, Herr Hellman. You're right."

Mark smiled at the professor and as his old teacher reached for the doorknob, he stopped his hand.

"We're gonna be fine," he said.

The professor tried to return his smile, but the attempt was weak. He left the room. Kathy was dressed when Mark returned and sat on the edge of the bed.

"What was that all about?" she said.

"I'll tell you in the shower."

* * *

Reginald Astair was in a fine mood at breakfast. He was waiting for them in the lobby, where the breakfast was served, when they came downstairs. Mark had to note that his attitude was in direct competition with everyone else.

"I've got a grand feeling about today," Reginald said. "We're going to make history, and it all begins with this historic walk."

The professor stirred his porridge silently. Mark and Kathy tried to look as enthusiastic as possible. They set out for the Antonia Fortress, the beginning of the painful way, as soon as they finished eating.

Fortress was an appropriate name for Herod's ancient military barracks. It was a massive structure, where Jesus was said to have been sentenced to death by Pontius Pilate. On four corners, massive stone turrets rose into the sky, casting long shadows on the sandy road on which the four travelers approached. In the East wall, the arches of the Lion's Gate loomed before them as the beginning of their journey. The leopards that guard the cavernous hole in the fortress wall stared down at them menacingly, and everyone seemed to be affected by them except for their expressionless bodyguards.

CHAPTER 9:

The professor kept a running commentary as they walked.

"This is where he was supposed to have met Simon of Cyrene, although I should mention that Pope Clement VI was the first to confirm this story in the fourteenth century, and we all know how little faith we are putting in the Catholic Church for the purposes of our truth-seeking."

Where Jesus was supposed to have met the man instructed by the Romans to carry his cross, there was now a stall selling magazines that claimed to detail the most sordid details of the lives of Israeli celebrities. The four travelers did not respond to the salesman as he waved his glossy-covered books in their faces. Ms. Copperfield clung to the arm of Herrn Hellman as they walked. There were other groups of people who were walking the route too. Most of these were religious groups. Walking the path was a common attraction for those who feel they can get closer to God by following in Jesus' footsteps.

Mark thought nothing of the group of men who walked behind them for the better part of a mile. There were many groups about, and until they acted, he had no reason to suspect that they were up to anything. But they were. It all happened very quickly. Shots rang out and before either of Reginald's bodyguards could make a move, their bodies hit the dirt, and puffs of sand flew up from the ground. One of them had nearly drawn his gun and it fell to the ground unfired. Reginald was shoved rudely to the ground, and the professor, Kathy, and Mark were grabbed by the shoulders. A Land Rover zoomed up the street, scattering the faithful in every direction, and the door swung open. The three travelers were thrown in the backseat and the door was slammed. The Land Rover sped away at an incredible speed and two guns, one from the back seat and one from the front, were trained on Mark, Kathy and the Professor. The man in the back seat, who had shoved Mark into the car, removed his mask and smiled at them.

"Welcome aboard, my friends," he laughed. The men up front laughed with him and Mark was chilled to the bone with fear.

They were instructed not to speak, and when Kathy disobeyed her head was struck with the butt of a pistol and fell forward. Mark tried to reach for her, but he found the barrel of a gun pressed into his temple.

"She'll be fine, loverboy. Just taking a nap. Why don't you take a cue from your friend here." He nodded at the professor, who sat with his hands in his lap and his head down, looking dejected at his decision to leave his art dealing for this.

"You've stolen us away from a very powerful man," Mark said. "You'll regret this."

"I doubt it," he said, and hit Mark on the skull. It all went black.

When Mark awoke his wrists were bound behind his back and he breathed in musty air. He was underground. There was a small barred window at what would have been eye-level if he was able to stand. He blinked and his eyes slowly adjusted to the dim lighting. He could see that he was in a cell with a dirt floor and three dirt walls. The bars in front of him were the only part of his cell that was not made of earth. Across from him was the professor, only separated from him by said iron bars. The professor looked like he was asleep. Mark certainly hoped he was asleep when he considered what the other options were.

Mark tried to stand up but found that he had been bound in a way to make that particular maneuver very painful. He cried out and found his way back to the floor. He wriggled across the cell and coughed the dust out of his mouth as he worked his way across the floor. He had to stop and rest every few feet. It was hard going. He was proud of himself when he reached the bars, but when he looked up from the ground he found that he was looking at his own reflection some very shiny black boots.

"Hello," a voice purred smoothly. "Herr...Hellman."

The voice laughed mirthlessly. Mark heard a key clink into a lock.

CHAPTER 10:

Mark was dragged down a hallway and into a room. He was incapable of walking while bound and his captors did not deign to untie him. He was hoisted up onto a chair that was bolted to the ground. It was incredibly painful to remain sitting on the chair as his bound hands and feet forced him to maintain the fetal position. He was cruelly made to get up again and again and attempt to sit in the chair. Two men wearing masks did this to him. After what could have been a year to Mark, but was more like ten minutes in real time, a voice from the corner spoke out.

"Enough. Let him stay down."

Mark couldn't see, but his intuition told him that the voice came from his left, and once he was able to focus his senses through the pain he could smell harsh, unfiltered, cigarette smoke wafting towards his nostrils from that direction. The owner of the voice and the cigarette smoke kneeled down next to Mark, but Mark was facing away. He remained that way. The man rolled him over and Mark groaned.

"I'm sorry you had to go through that," the man said. "It's an exercise we do here. It tends to make people more..." He twirled his cigarette in the air, searching for the words in a mock-serious manner. "Pliable."

"Can't imagine why," Mark grunted.

The man laughed a terrible throaty laugh that made him choke. He leaned forward on his knees and coughed.

"So he's got a sense of humor," he said. "He maintains that. Maybe he also maintains what he's doing in my city."

"You don't own this city," Mark said.

"Ah, my archaeologist friend, that is where you are wrong. I very much do own this city." He gauged Mark's face for a reaction. "Yes," he said. "I know who you are. I am not in the business of capturing people I am not deeply interested in."

"That is very generous of you."

"Again, thank you. Your sense of humor is truly inspiring. But don't you wonder why you are here?"

"I've been kidnapped so many times lately that it's beginning to lose interest for me."

The man looked at his associates, who stood by the door with their arms crossed. They nodded in agreement with him.

"So Reggie grabbed you, did he?" He laughed some more and Mark wished more than anything that this man would never laugh in his presence again. It was a truly haunting noise. "I would have thought he'd moved past that. He claims to be so...evolved, these days. Typical."

"You know Mr. Astair?"

"Mr. Astair? How proper of you, though I can assure you your friend does not deserve the formality. Yes. I know Reggie. We go way back in fact. I am...as he would put it, also a seeker."

"The grail?"

"Obviously," the man muttered, showing his first signs of annoyance. "Did you really imagine that your obsession with the grail would go unnoticed? You're quite brilliant."

"It did go unnoticed."

"By some, yes," he said, taking the final drag of his cigarette and tossing it away. "But not the faithful."

"Gentlemen," he said to the other men. "Let's give Mr. Lockheed the chance to get cleaned up. I want to see him in my dining room at six thirty."

"What about my friends?" Mark said, as the man was walking out of the room. He looked at Mark over his shoulder.

"We will discuss that over some Shakshouka and of course a lovely Merlot from your own country's fine Napa Valley. See you then, Mr. Lockheed," he bowed and exited the room.

The two men walked towards him to cut his ties.

CHAPTER 11:

"It's really very simple," the man purred. Mark now knew that his name was Gabriel Mizrahi. Mark had been brought to a bathroom to clean up and given soft linen clothing. He grudgingly had to admit that he was terribly comfortable in them after the abuse he had received at the hands of these men. "I need you to work for me instead, but not for the grail."

"You don't want the grail? But I thought –" then Gabriel interrupted him.

"I want the grail. Do not misunderstand me. But there are other things I want. And I think you can help me."

"I don't know what you're talking about."

"The burial shroud, Mr. Lockheed, for starters. And the crown of thorns. Along with the cup of Christ, they make up the trinity. The owner of all three is the master of death."

"You don't believe this? You can't master death."

Gabriel Mizrahi stared across the long oaken table at Mark very evenly. He did believe it.

"What I believe is neither here nor there. But I am quite sure your Mr. Astair is seeking the same trinity. He is of a different mind, let's say, about which should be found first. The shroud must come first...for very practical reasons."

"And what reasons are those?"

"You don't want to inquire about your fee first?"

"You were planning on paying me?"

"Mr. Lockheed," he said, taking a sip of his wine after letting it swirl around in his glass. "Do I look like a monster?" He smiled wide at Mark. "Of course I'll pay you, and your friends."

"And if we don't succeed?"

"I believe you know the answer to that."

He did, and he didn't fancy dying.

"So tell me, Mr. Mizrahi, why the shroud first?"

Gabriel Mizrahi proceeded to tell Mark a story. It was a story about a dedicated Jewish archaeologist in the 1930s. Mr. Mizrahi neglected to mention that this man was his grandfather, but Mark would eventually put the pieces together. This archaeologist was searching for the burial shroud of Christ. The man was Jewish in name only, and like most archaeologists, was a secular at heart. But he held a deep and mystical fascination with the trinity of Christ's effects, one that he would pass on to his son, and eventually to his grandson. He made great inroads to finding the shroud in the early years of the 1930s, and he believed that he had it pinned down to a specific location. He was under the impression that the shroud of Christ had become a family heirloom, and had made its way to Europe with one of many Jewish families that had made their way there over the centuries. He was very close to pinpointing the location of the shroud, when Hitler rose to power. Gabriel Mizrahi believed that like so many other priceless antiquities, the shroud had been taken from a Jewish family by officers of the SS as a bribe that they had no intention of completing the deal on. And like most of those antiquities, it was still sitting in a bank vault in Switzerland. Or so Gabriel Mizrahi believed.

"I would think that would make it the least urgent of the three," Mark said skeptically.

"But that is where you are wrong," Gabriel said. "You do not pay enough attention to the news in your little hole in the Pentagon. The filthy Swiss are finally losing their battle in the courts. There are appeals, but it will not be long before the vaults are thrown open and made to subject themselves to a new disclosure obligation . That cannot happen to the shroud. I will never find it then. It must be before that. I can live with some long since forgotten Van Gogh being returned to the heirs of its rightful owners, but the shroud is mine. And it comes first."

"And Mr. Astair?"

"He can take care of himself."

"My friends are okay?"

"They are in much better shape than you, I assure you."

"Then let's discuss logistics."

31

CHAPTER 12:

"You can't be serious?" The professor was pacing around the room. It was the room that Mark had been moved to when he had been given clothes and the chance to take a shower. "We just take him at his word?"

"Oh, of course not," Mark said. "I don't trust him for a minute. But the way I see it, we don't have much of a choice."

Kathy was sitting with her back to the door and her hands steepled in front of her face, covering her mouth. She lowered them to speak.

"Mark is right. What happens if we say no?"

"Nothing good," the professor muttered. "Two days ago I was selling knockoffs and planning my next stroll through the red light district. It wasn't a glamorous life, but it was safer than this shit."

"I can sympathize with that, Professor, but here we are. This is what we're living with right now."

"So I guess we're going to Switzerland then?" Kathy said, standing up. She walked across to where the professor was pacing, and Mark stood with his arms nonchalantly crossed in front of his chest. She unfolded his arms and placed them around her shoulders before kissing and hugging him tenderly. Mark didn't tell her how much it hurt to hug her. Neither of them knew what had been done to him, and he didn't plan on telling them.

Mark released Kathy, and left one arm draped over her. They both turned to the professor who came towards them. They went into a huddle.

"We're in this together," Mark said. They all agreed.

Gabriel Mizrahi had a plane as well. The twin-engine turboprop plane was not nearly as luxurious as Reginald Astair's plane, but it was a plane. Mark watched through the tiny and grimed-over window as it roared into life and soon they were airborne.

Mr. Mizrahi informed them that he had a contact in Geneva who would be meeting them at the tarmac.

"He is our best bet to get inside Credit Suisse," he explained. "Seeing as he used to work there."

"And?" Kathy asked.

"Let's just say he ran into a spot of personal trouble and he no longer works there."

"Let's just," the professor muttered, stroking his graying facial stubble.

"Anyway," Mr. Mizrahi continued. "Getting something out of a Swiss vault undetected is no easy job, and certainly isn't one for an archaeologist. So we'll need some help. You will, of course, be in charge of confirming the authenticity of the shroud once we have it." He spoke as if it were inevitability that they would find out which vault the shroud was in, and could break in and retrieve it without being caught.

"All we can really do is telling you if it's from the correct time period," Kathy said.

"I'll know the rest," Gabriel said dreamily. "Trust me. I'll know it."

Mark found the man's faith in the trinity of Christ's personal effects moving, but disturbing.

The rest of the flight with its two stopovers for refueling was uneventful, but relatively loud. Mark took solace in the breathtaking views of the Alps afforded to him by his small window. It sure beat the views from the hole back at the Pentagon. He wondered what the people in the hole were doing while he flew above the Alps with Kathy, his old college professor, and an Israeli madman. Whatever it was, he reasoned, it wasn't as invigorating or exciting as this. Mark was scared, but he was alive.

CHAPTER 13:

They didn't know where Mr. Mizrahi was taking them. Geneva wasn't like other European cities that Mark and Kathy had been to on location. It made London seem like a backwater country town by comparison. Mark had never seen so many people in one place. The streets were ringing with bicycle bells, because everybody seemed to feel compelled to use them all the time. They crossed the street running through dangerously tiny breaks in traffic on the road. The citizens walking on the sidewalk and on their cell phones seemed to take no notice of the chaos around them.

Gabriel Mizrahi bullied his way through the crowd, shouldering and elbowing passers-by out of the way when necessary.

It seemed to the professor, (who shouted it above the din in Mark's ear) that they were headed to a not so pleasant neighborhood. Even the crowd began to thin out after a while, and eventually they found themselves accompanied by only the occasional lost soul. Only then did Mr. Mizrahi slow down.

"Where are we?" Mark said.

"The Jewish quarter," he said. "The ghetto created for Jews that were in Switzerland during the war. It has never really recovered. People say that there is a bad smell in the air, or that the buildings are haunted."

"What do you think?" Mark asked.

"I think..." he paused. "I think my associate lives here and that we need to talk to him."

It was obvious to Mark that Gabriel was holding something else back, but he didn't push it. Gabriel Mizrahi had made a very clear impression on Mark in a short amount of time, and he did not give the impression of a man who should be pushed. Mark would just have to wait for his answers.

When they reached a low-slung building with blacked-out windows, Gabriel consulted a sheet of paper from his pocket and then knocked quietly.

The door opened just a crack and a pair of eyes looked out at them.

"Is that you Gabriel?"

"Can't you see it's me, Snead?" Mizrahi responded.

"I don't see well in the light anymore. What was the name of our rabbi when we were ten?"

"Schulman."

"What was his first name?"

"For fuck's sake I don't remember his first name will you open the door?"

The man who Mr. Mizrahi called Snead opened the door but paused after Gabriel entered and looked warily at his companions.

"They're with me," Gabriel said. "They're the whole reason I've come to see you, now let them in."

It was the strangest apartment Mark had ever seen. There was no furniture but some scattered pillows. There was a candle burning in the middle of the room on the floor with a lampshade carefully placed over it as if to dim its already sparse light. The whole room was bathed in a depressing shade of darkness. It was not utterly dark, but only enough light from the candle escaped to illuminate the worst qualities of life.

"Don't let them disturb anything," the man said as he closed the door and fastened seven locks one by one. Mark couldn't imagine what there was to be disturbed.

Snead was a fidgety man who wore a dirty bathrobe and thick socks. He had the shadow of a beard, so Mark figured he must own a razor or groom himself in some way. He constantly rubbed the side of his nose with his grimy fingers.

"Aren't you going to invite us to sit down?" Gabriel said. "Though I see you're a little low on furniture right now. Pawn it all?"

"Maybe," the man replied. "Do you have anything for me?"

"I might," Gabriel purred, his interest piqued. "If you can get me in touch with some good plumbing contractors."

"Hard to come by...some left...arrested...or gone legit," the man stuttered unevenly.

"Oh I'm sure," Mizrahi continued unfazed, "You could rustle up somebody. What do you say?"

Mr. Mizrahi reached into his pocket and pulled out a small plastic bag.

"Well," Snead said. "Luc might be in town. He could know of a few others. You might get a decent crew together from that. What kind of plumbing are we talking about? Big job?"

"The biggest."

"And these ones fit into this somehow?" he motioned at Kathy, Mark, and Dr. LeTrec, who were lined up one by one against the wall. There was nothing else to lean against.

"I'm not at liberty to comment on that."

"You always did play it close to the chest. Now...may I?" he said, reaching for the bag still in Gabriel's hand. Gabriel drew it away.

"First, I believe you have a phone call to make for me."

"Of course, of course," Snead muttered, walking out of his dingy living room and into a kitchen that Mark didn't imagine could look much worse.

"Trust me," Mr. Mizrahi said, turning to his companions once Snead had left the room.

"Do we have a choice?" Mark said.

"That's a good boy."

CHAPTER 14:

The professor and Kathy waited in the car. It was a Renault, parked across the street from the cafe where Mark and Mr. Mizrahi were to meet Luc. If Luc had a last name, it had not been made evident. Kathy could just see Mark's head above the roof of a parked car, through the cafe's front windows.

"His head is bobbing," the professor said. "Is he nodding at someone? Did this guy show up?"

"No," Kathy said. "He's just nervous. He's tapping his feet too I bet."

The professor drummed his fingers on the headrest of Kathy's seat. It began to rain. First it was a drizzle, but it slowly progressed until it was a full-fledged downpour. There was no hope of seeing anything that was going on in the cafe.

"Why do you think we weren't allowed?"

"This again? We've gone over and over this, I don't know, Kathy. Roll with the punches here. I thought you archaeologists were great at getting kidnapped and forced to do missions. I've seen movies."

"Hilarious, but seriously. How does it not bother you that we have to miss this?"

"Of course it bothers me, now shut up about it. I'm just not trying to think too much about it."

A man came up and knocked on the driver's side window loudly. He rapped his knuckles against the window pane again and again. He had a dark beard and from the noise his fists were making he must have been wearing several rings. If Kathy hadn't been wearing her seatbelt she might have skyrocketed into the ceiling of the car and concussed herself, that's how shocked she was by the noise at first.

"Shit," the professor said, drumming the headrest with his fingers again.

"What? What does he want?"

"He thinks we're a damn cab," he said.

They were in a yellow SUV that had appeared at their hotel that morning. Gabriel had hopped in since he had had the keys nobody dared to ask any questions.

"Well tell him to go away," Kathy said.

"Why don't you? I'm not opening a window in this weather."

"Christ," she muttered.

She leaned across the center console, pushed the button for a split second, cracking the window only a little. Rain still gushed in the crack in the window and pooled in the driver's seat. Mr. Mizrahi would be happy about that.

"We're not a fucking cab," she yelled, and pushed the up button. "Think that'll make him go away?"

"It ought a," the professor said.

Suddenly a crowbar crashed through the driver's side window, spraying Kathy with shards of glass and droplets of water that were indistinguishable from each other only by the lack of blood drawn by the water. A gloved hand reached in and unlocked the door. Kathy and the professor were both too stunned to do anything. The man got the door open and closed it behind him. He unlocked the car and another man got in the back seat with the professor.

"You folks staying or leaving?" the second man cackled, showing his yellowing teeth, nearly the same color as the car.

Kathy and the professor fled out of the car and watched helplessly from the curb as it drove away, leaving a trail of broken glass in its wake.

CHAPTER 15:

"So what's this guy like?" Mark said, sipping his espresso that Gabriel had told him to order. "You always order something, even if you don't drink it," he had said. "You must look like a normal customer."

"But as far as I know...I am a normal customer," Mark had said. "And I don't like espresso."

Gabriel had ordered him an espresso anyway.

"He's good at his job," Mr. Mizrahi said.

"Which is?"

Gabriel Mizrahi just stared at Mark and sipped his espresso. Gabriel Mizrahi happened to love espresso, and he relished it. The cafe was quite good. There was some kind of ruckus outside. They thought they had heard the sound of a window breaking and glass hitting pavement, but it was raining so hard they couldn't see anything out of the fogged cafe windows. They sat in silence after several attempts by Mark to start a conversation. Gabriel wouldn't even discuss grail lore. He was on edge, and Mark didn't like it when a man like Gabriel was on edge. That meant this Luc character was "good enough at his job" to scare Gabriel.

It was obvious that the man they were waiting for had arrived when he came through the door. He was an enormous man, closer to seven feet than six, and he wore a turban on his head, making him appear even taller. His beard was full and thick, with a few gray hairs showing. His jaw was iron set, carved from stone. He nodded at Gabriel and came to their table. He pulled a chair up from another table, and before Mark could tell him that they had already saved him a chair, he pushed it up against another chair and sat across both of them as a normal sized man would have sat across one.

"You are looking well Gabriel," the man said in a soft voice that belied his size. "Though tired, I must admit."

Mark could not place the man's accent, but it was not European.

"I trust I find you well too, Luc?" Gabriel said.

"Allah, blessed be his name, has been kind to me. Some others of the old crew not so much. What brings you to Swiss soil?"

"An errand."

"Isn't it always an errand with you? Who's your friend?"

"I am not his friend," Mark said, extending his hand. The man looked surprised but received it cordially. "And my name is of no consequence, but you may call me M."

The man laughed a deep belly laugh, and he seemed to shake the whole restaurant. He slapped his hand on the table and Mark could feel the eyes on them from all around. The waiter came running and asked if he could get anything for the newcomer. Luc ordered an Amandine and sent the waiter away.

"So your young friend thinks he is a spy, Gabriel? You make me laugh bringing a man like this. What is this errand?"

"This man is useful to me. That's all that matters. And I wanted you to be familiar with his face...so that you don't blow it off when the time comes. I'd like his head to remain where it is."

"And a pretty one it is isn't it?" Luc licked his lips and laughed again, less heartily this time. "Is it a typical arrangement you are looking for?"

"Yes. Nothing else. You don't need to get bogged down with details. I can give you a place to be and a wire transfer."

"I want double what I had in Prague."

"Done," Gabriel said. He stood up and beckoned Mark to follow him. They did not shake hands or say goodbye to Luc, but walked out of the cafe and into the rain. Gabriel seemed to want to put as much distance between himself and Luc as he could. He was carrying an umbrella under his arm, Mark could see that, but he didn't open it in his rush.

Gabriel stopped suddenly. He was staring, open-mouthed at the curb across the street. The professor and Kathy were standing there looking dumbfounded. Kathy's face was bleeding.

Mark ran across the street, was narrowly missed by several cars, and went to inquire of Kathy's health. Mr. Mizrahi impatiently pressed the crosswalk button and breathed heavily in anger.

CHAPTER 16:

"That fuck set us up," Gabriel said before Kathy and the professor could stutter apologies. "Shit!" he screamed and kicked a piece of glass that had once been a part of his car window and sent it careening into the street. "Come on," he said. "We'll walk. It'll be good for us."

They walked the eleven blocks back to the hotel and Mr. Mizrahi asked them all to come to his room. It was nothing like the rooms the rest of them were staying in. This room that was actually a suite had a fountain, a sparkling chandelier and three bathrooms. They sat around a fireplace in the living room and Gabriel started rubbing his temples.

"That was my fault," he said. "What happened today. I got sloppy. I trust the two of you are okay?"

Kathy and the professor nodded, surprised at the concerned tone in Mr. Mizrahi's voice.

"I promised that you would not be harmed in this and I am a man of my word. Know that, if you know anything. I do not go back on my word."

"So," Mark said. "What happened?" He said what all of them were thinking.

"Luc does not appreciate it when I bring uncovered women with me to our little transactions. He knows that I always oblige him. So I asked Kathy to stay in the car."

"What about me?" the professor said.

"You're both Frenchmen. I just didn't want to deal with that. But he clearly had us followed before the meeting. He knew I was with a woman and that I'd leave her in the car. And he had some of his pals steal it from me."

"What for?"

"To piss me off."

"So it's off then? Whatever you want him to do?"

"What?" Gabriel said, genuinely shocked at the suggestion. "Of course not. He's the best. We say nothing about his little surprise. The two of you have my sincerest apologies. Now," he said. "If you'll excuse me."

He walked to his hotel phone and dialed a number.

"Yes, Sabrina please if you can. No, not Cynthia, I've always had Sabrina. Yes I know. Well I'll pay more just cancel that one. Yes. Thank you. Of course." He held his hand to the mouthpiece of the phone and gave them an annoyed look with a wave of his hand. He mouthed "out" and they filed out together, to return to their much less impressive rooms.

Kathy insisted that she wanted to do nothing but go to bed, so Mark and his old professor went down to the hotel lobby to drink some tea and mull over the events of the day, and whatever the future might hold

"Remember when we were academics?" the professor said, stirring sugar into his Earl Grey. "Where everything was delightfully hypothetical and fit nicely between the margins. What happened to that?"

"We should have gone into linguistics," Mark said humorlessly. "Nothing but words all day. Couldn't be too bad."

"Sounds awful," the professor said, and they both laughed.

"Fair enough. So is getting carjacked all it's hyped up to be?"

The front desk clerk gave them a curious look, but immediately turned her eyes back to her TV drama.

"Everything and more, my boy. Though I imagine that's probably not the last of our excitement on this trip, eh?"

"Somehow I think not," Mark said. "Somehow I think not."

CHAPTER 17:

The phone in Kathy and Mark's room rang early in the morning. Kathy groaned and reached over Mark to pick up the receiver. The voice on the other end was familiar and low and the sound of it woke Kathy up immediately. She set the phone down and shook Mark awake.

"You need to take the phone," she said.

"Hello, Mark. How are you?" It was Reginald Astair. "Don't panic this call is safe. I've been careful."

"Where are you calling from right now?"

"I can't tell you that."

"What can you tell me?"

"That I'll be around. I'll be watching. Be ready. I can't tell you when or where you'll be, but there will be a time, when I'll be there, and I'll rescue you. Then we can get back to doing what we set out to do. Do you understand?"

"Yes," Mark said robotically.

"Good."

After a click and the line went dead and Mark explained to Kathy what Reginald had said.

"Should we tell the professor?" she said.

"Maybe...but not yet," Mark said. "Not unless he got a call of his own. I think we play this one close to the chest."

"We seem to be getting pretty good at that."

"We're getting pretty good at something else too."

"Oh yeah?" she said, rolling over on her back and biting the tip of her pinky finger. "And what's that?"

Mark swam through the ocean of sheets to join her.

* * *

They had a meeting in Mr. Mizrahi's room that morning after breakfast, where he told them what they had to do that day. Obviously it was set to be an amazing day.

"I've assembled the rest of the team we will need," he said. "You already know Luc, but stealing from a Swiss bank vault is no easy task. Today, we have to make a quick trip to Montreux to get something very important."

"What's that?" Mark said.

"Our uniforms."

* * *

Gabriel had arranged for a new method of travel for them. Since there car had been stolen the day before, he had evidently not been wasting his time. There were two sleek, black Ducatis waiting for them with the valet when they went outside. The professor was to ride with Mr. Mizrahi, and Kathy with Mark. Mark accepted the helmet from the valet and pulled it down over his head. He flipped up the sun-visor and watched as Kathy climbed onto the bike, her helmet already on.

"You coming?" she said. She revved the engine and made it clear that she was driving.

Mark hopped on.

"Hold on tight," she said. And he did. He wrapped his arms around her small midsection and they were off.

There is perhaps no better country to ride through on a motorcycle than Switzerland. They rode over mountain passes and on winding roads, where the mountain air was crisp as it streamed over the top of their helmets and shoulders. At one point, far ahead of Gabriel and the professor, Kathy stopped the bike at a particularly beautiful spot. She pulled over to the side and took her helmet off, placing it in her lap. The tops of the fir trees swayed in the breeze while below them Lac Léman sparkled in the sun. A bird was flying high in the sky and dove down for an animal that they couldn't see.

Kathy turned and pulled Mark's helmet off his head. He smiled at her.

"Isn't it beautiful?" she said.

"Yes," Mark replied, not looking at their surroundings, but straight into her eyes.

Kathy took Mark's face in her hands, the roughness pleasant against her palms, and kissed him deeply. It was over quickly, the moment only fleeting, before they had to get back on the road. They took one more look at the view of the mountains and the lake, and put their helmets back on, leaving the idyllic moment they had shared just where it had been before they had stumbled upon it.

CHAPTER 18:

After a while Mr. Mizrahi and the professor caught up with Mark and Kathy and after approximately two hours, Mr. Mizrahi motioned to follow him off an exit ramp. When they got to the bottom of the ramp, Mark couldn't help but notice that there was nothing around. Well, nearly nothing. There was a stadium sized, corrugated steel-sided warehouse that looked as if it hadn't been used in decades.

"Here we are," Gabriel said.

"Here?" Kathy said, vocalizing Mark and the professor's thoughts as well.

"Yep," Gabriel said. "This is the place. Absolutely crucial."

They got off the bikes and walked all the way around the building to a small door that Gabriel had a key for in his motorcycle jacket. He was the type of man who always seemed to have the right key for the right moment. The key took some jiggling, but after a moment the door creaked open, and motion sensors switched on high power fluorescents overhead. Mark couldn't see what they had driven several hours for. The warehouse didn't have anything in it but boxes. The back half of the warehouse was cardboard boxes from floor to ceiling. This is where Gabriel was heading without further explanation. They could hear the scurrying of mice that were unaccustomed to being disturbed as they walked.

When they reached the stacks of boxes Gabriel began opening them, seemingly at random.

"Nope," he said. "Nope. Not this one. Warmer, but no."

Kathy, Mark, and the professor walked behind Gabriel and peeked into the boxes that he had opened, and what they saw was surprising. In each box was a different uniform. One box contained United States Postal Services uniforms. Another contained clown costumes. One was stuffed full of green barista aprons. Mark was horrified to see in one box, the winged uniforms of nearly every major international airline. This went on for the better part of an hour before Gabriel finally threw up his hands in victory.

"Voilà!"

What Gabriel had finally found was a box of uniforms of a specific bank in Geneva, Switzerland. There were the uniforms for tellers complete with pinned ascot, the ties and tie clips necessary for advisors and managers, with the appropriate name tags, and there was one for the security guards. Gabriel had to rummage around the boxes near at hand to find another security guard outfit: he was looking for the biggest one he could find. He instructed Mark to choose a tie and tie clip, Kathy to pick out a teller's uniform. Only the professor got left out.

"Nothing? If I could end up spending my life in a Swiss prison, I'd really like to be involved at least," he said.

"You'll be involved," Mr. Mizrahi said. "You're going to be outside running the show. Don't worry about your involvement."

When they had their new uniforms packed neatly away in their motorcycle side bags, they got back on their cycles and headed back to Geneva. Before they left, the professor nagged again:

"It's been a long trip. Can we stop and get some food on the way back?"

Gabriel Mizrahi stared at the professor as if he had asked a considerably more absurd question. Gabriel looked off into the distance and squinted. Mark got the feeling he was looking for something specific and he couldn't help but thinking of the phone call he and Kathy had received in their room that morning.

"No," Gabriel said. "We can't."

CHAPTER 19:

The day of the motorcycle trip was two days before the planned bank heist. How he was so sure this was the correct bank, Gabriel would not share, but only repeatedly say:

"It's the one."

Mark mused that confidence must be very important in Gabriel's line of work.

For the first time, Gabriel left them completely out of the loop the next day, as he went to do some planning with the other members of the team. Evidently, there were two other people, besides Luc, who would be involved in the operation. Mark was of the mind that keeping things simple is usually the best way to go, but he kept his mouth shut. He and Kathy stayed in bed for most of the morning, but got out of bed around noon. Kathy went down to the hotel library and came back a few minutes later. Mark was sitting in an armchair, drinking coffee, and had the news on the TV, muted.

"Look at this," Kathy said. She was holding a book. It was Mysteries of the Holy Grail, by Marcus Watters.

Mark smirked at her.

"Watters? You're joking, right? Surely you know that he's a hack of the lowest orders."

"Of course I know that. Everyone who has ever spent ten minutes with you knows how much you hate Marcus Watters."

"I almost punched him at an archaeology convention in Boston."

"I actually heard about that. But that's exactly my point. I picked it up because it occurred to me that you would pick it up too."

"Probably to hide it behind another book. Any other book."

"Well when I picked it up, something fell out."

She waved a small, torn piece of notebook paper in her hand. Mark stood up so quickly he nearly spilled his coffee all over his boxers and legs.

"What is it?"

"A note. For you."

"Who is it from?"

"It doesn't say."

She handed him the note.

Mr. Lockheed,

What an honor to have you in Switzerland. If you have found this, you live up to your reputation. They say that you always see more than meets the eye? Let us see if that is quite as true as some would have me believe.

Cordially

"No name?"

"Not unless cordially is a name. And it isn't. That I know of."

Mark involuntarily scratched his chin. Part of him longed for the hole, for people to think poorly of him again. He didn't always like this newfound status, where everyone thought he was so clever. It was so much easier under the radar than having to live up to other's expectations.

"So?" Kathy said.

"So what?"

"Who is it from?"

"I have no idea."

"But the note says you have a reputation."

"The note vastly overestimates my cleverness."

He handed the scrap of paper back to Kathy and went back to his coffee. He turned the volume up on the news. There had been a bombing in Jerusalem, but that wasn't really anything new.

CHAPTER 20:

The day of the heist dawned like any other. The sun shone in the blinds of Mark and Kathy's hotel room. Kathy woke up and Mark was pacing the room nervously. She looked at the clock on the bedside table and saw that it read 5:30.

"We don't have to get up for another hour," she said. "Come back to bed."

"Do you think the bank manager is asleep right now?" Mark said. "No, he's not."

Mark had a very specific image in his head of a blonde-haired, impeccable suit-wearing Swiss man going about his early morning routine, doing an absurd amount of safety checks. He went coolly about his business; calm in the assurance of his banks many safety protocols. He went about his business because he had to, because it was what he did every morning, but he never imagined that anyone would actually attempt to breach them. Who would try to rob his bank? It was insanity. Complete madness.

"It's insanity," Mark said. "Complete madness. We're archaeologists Kathy, not bank robbers."

"Well," Kathy said. "To be fair, if the shroud is actually there. It doesn't belong to some rich guy who stuffed it in a secret bank vault."

"It belongs in a museum," Mark said. "And I don't think that's what Gabriel has in mind."

Mark continued to pace the room. He wasn't really pacing because he was nervous, or because of the image he had in his head of the Swiss bank manager doing his morning rounds. It was because of guilt. He felt guilty because he wanted to do this. He wanted to do if for entirely selfish reasons. He wanted to do it because it brought him one step closer to the grail. That was what he had set out on this trip for wasn't it? The grail. And if this was what he had to do...then so be it.

"What are you thinking?" Kathy said.

"That I should be more hesitant about this."

"You're not?"

"No, I mean I am. It's nuts. But it's exhilarating. And Gabriel is a loon, but he wants the grail too. How incredible would it be to actually find it? To find the shroud and the crown of thorns too?"

"You can't actually believe that we'll accomplish that? I know you understand science...the conditions that would be required for that crown to have survived relatively unscathed until now. It's not likely."

"But it's possible. And that's all I can think about. And I feel guilty about it."

"Come back to bed," Kathy said again. And this time, Mark reluctantly did.

* * *

The professor was having a very similar morning, but was forced to go through it alone. He too was going through a roller coaster of emotions and found it impossible to sleep. He too paced his room in his underwear and peeked out the blinds at the city below. Everyone was going about their business as if nothing out of the ordinary was to occur. They didn't know. How could they? To them it was just another day. Another day to buy groceries and take their kids to the park and open their windows to let a breeze roll in while they made Roesti for lunch.

The professor went to his hotel phone more frantically than was necessary. He picked it up and listened to the recording explaining which buttons he had to push for international calls. He pushed the buttons and then dialed Karen's number from memory. Karen was his wife. They were separated, had been for several years. At some point his drinking had become too much for her. She had been the first one to tell him that he needed to cut back or the university was going to do something about it.

"The people are talking," she had told him one morning over her coffee. "And if you don't get it together you could lose your job. I'm telling you this for your own sake."

But he hadn't listened and she had left before it all went downhill, but she had left all the same.

The phone rang and rang in her parlor somewhere outside of Detroit. She was living a man named Robert now. He knew that. It was Robert who answered the phone.

"It's Claude."

There was a silence on the line that he had wholly expected.

"Why are you calling?"

"Please just let me talk to her. It will only be a second."

There was some shuffling and the professor could hear that Robert had set the receiver down. He heard him call for Karen and he relaxed, took a deep breath.

"Hello," she said tentatively. "Claude?"

"Hello, Karen."

"Is everything alright?"

After years apart and though they were thousands of miles away from each other, she could tell there was a problem. She could read it in the desperate tone of his voice.

"I just wanted to say that I'm sorry. I was wrong all along. I have a problem and I know that now. I always knew deep down but I didn't want to admit it, and I'm sorry. I guess I just called to say that I'm very sorry for everything I put you through. You should just know that. I wanted you to know that."

"Well...thank you," she said. "Are you sure everything's alright? You sound flustered. Are you in some kind of trouble?"

"No. I just wanted to make amends. Take care, Karen."

"Wait," she said, but he had hung up the phone.

He could move forward with a clearer head now. He got in the shower to prepare for the day.

* * *

Gabriel Mizrahi had had no trouble sleeping at all. He had slept like a lamb and was up with the dawn, well-rested and raring to go. He had never felt so refreshed in his life. He was more confident than ever that it was going to be the most glorious day of his entire existence and not just his thirty year quest. All of his ducks were in a row. Everyone had been briefed on what their assignment was their part in the operation. It was true that there were going to be many moving parts, perhaps too many, but Gabriel didn't think so. They were a determined lot, and they ought to be, he thought. He had gathered them again in his suite late the night before and had taken his time, given careful instructions. The others had sat in near silence for three hours while he explained in turn what each of them was to do. They had all accepted without question. And now the day had come.

He looked at himself in the bathroom mirror and he liked what he saw. He saw a man who was, before long, to become the most powerful man in the world.

CHAPTER 21:

They rode silently in the car together. The professor and Kathy sat in the back while Mark sat in the passenger seat and Gabriel drove. Mark wore his blue suit with the tie and tie clip indicating that he worked for the bank. Gabriel wore street clothes; jeans and a button up shirt. Kathy wore the teller's uniform. She nervously tugged at the ascot around her neck as if it was a noose and she was being strangled by it. They were to park the car in the bank's employee parking deck across the street. Nobody knew how Gabriel had gotten his hands on the sticker that was affixed to the van's front windshield to indicate their employee status. He was not a man prone to over-explaining and the others had to live with it.

When they were exiting the van and the professor was unfolding the laptop that Gabriel had provided for him, Mark gave him a thumbs up and Kathy gave him her best attempt at a smile.

Mark and Kathy entered the bank at 7:34 am. It had been open for business for four minutes. None of them could have predicted how quickly everything went down. Luc nodded at them as they entered the building. He stood by the doors in his uniform they had brought from the warehouse two days before. Mark shuddered to think what dark alley the man who would normally stand there in the morning was crumpled in. He pushed it out of his mind. As they had been informed would be the case, there was an empty teller's slot closest to the door and a desk with a plaque that read: Markus Zeims, Client Relationship Manager, also closest to the door. The fate of these two bank employees was not something either Kathy or Mark wanted to consider. They simply did as they were told and took their places.

Mark sat down at the desk and loosened his tie. He logged onto the computer with the password 52302 as he had been instructed, and surfed the internet in an attempt to look as if he was busy. Kathy took her place at the teller's slot and held to faith that no one would bother her before Gabriel entered the bank. She could do nothing but stare at her increasingly sweaty hands.

Gabriel entered the bank at 7:41. He was listening to the professor through his earpiece. He informed him that all police scanners were clear. No one had had a loose tongue.

"Good," Gabriel said to himself.

Gabriel Mizrahi walked calmly up to the slot where Kathy stood and acted as if he had never met her before.

"Young lady," he said brusquely. "I need to get into my safe deposit box immediately."

"Sir, let me help you it will only take a moment," she said.

"Quickly please. I don't have all day."

Kathy picked up the phone from her station and dialed 4, which was the number for Mark's desk. They were not more than forty feet apart, but Mark picked up the phone.

"Mr.," she said into the phone. "Sir, what was your name?"

"Lundgren."

"Mr. Lundgren would like to get into his safe deposit box."

"Send him my way."

Kathy instructed Gabriel to see one of the relationship managers, Mr. Zeims. When Gabriel reached Mark's desk he offered his hand.

"Markus Lundgren," he said.

"A pleasure. I assume you have your codes sir?"

"Why certainly."

He handed Mark a piece of paper that was folded, and entirely blank. Mark looked at it and nodded.

"Very good. Right this way sir."

There was a loud conversation drifting across the bank lobby as Mark led Gabriel toward the vault. They had all been given blueprints of the bank by Gabriel at the last meeting and Mark had spent most of the night memorizing it. He didn't want to consider what would happen if he forgot. But in that moment it didn't matter because a gunshot rang out.

They turned and saw a man lying at Luc's feet. Evidently, he had known Luc from somewhere, and had asked him when he'd started working at the bank.

All hell broke loose at that point. Gabriel pulled out a gun and yelled at Mark.

"Go!"

They made their way to the vault. As they sprinted down the hallway a security officer yelled at them to halt. Mark froze. Gabriel coolly spun around and split the man's skull wide open with a .40 caliber bullet from his Desert Eagle Mk VII.

"Move," he said to Mark. Mark could only read his lips because his ears were ringing so badly.

"Where are they?" Mark said. He was referring to the other two men involved in the operation. They were supposed to come in once Mark and Gabriel were in the vault. The plan had been for Mark and Gabriel to reach the vault, and for Mark to 'realize' that he had forgotten his keycard. They would use the intercom to call up another client relationship manager to bring his keycard. Luc would shadow that person and before he would realize that Mark was not actually an employee at that bank, he would knock him out and take his keycard. Once in the vault, the other two men, who were the petemen, would break into the specific safe deposit box they were looking for.

Gabriel didn't answer. The professor spoke in his ear.

"All police units in a fifteen kilometer radius are out."

Luc came bounding up the hallway with a keycard no doubt taken from a dead body. He handed it to Gabriel who slid it and the doors automatically opened with a satisfying sound.

The vault was bigger than Mark could have ever imagined. On several levels Metal doors went from floor to ceiling with a bridge-like construction that led to an elevator across the room that Gabriel was heading for. Mark followed, while Luc stayed at the door. Mark had a hard time keeping his cool and wondered how everything had gone so terribly wrong so quickly.

Once in the caged elevator, Gabriel entered the number of safe deposit box #23765 so it would bring them there.

"How are we getting in?" Mark asked.

"The old fashioned way," Gabriel said.

When they reached the other floor, which was roughly forty feet in the air, Gabriel stared at it in awe for a moment. But he didn't waste much time. Mark could only watch in horror as he drew what could only be a detonator out of his messenger bag. After that, he pulled out a large chunk of orange colored putty, covered with a wrapper that said Semtex, before starting to spread the putty – that was actually plastic explosive – on the vault door.

"Always have a backup plan, Lockheed. Always."

"You're not going to detonate that?"

"Of course I am."

"But what about the shroud?"

Gabriel stopped, stood up and put his hands on Mark's shoulders.

"There is one thing I want you to remember, Mark Lockheed. If I can't have the trinity, nobody can."

It took him less than five minutes to have the explosive and the detonator affixed to the door and go back to the elevator. He pulled a cell phone from his pocket once they had reached the lower level.

Despite his feelings on religion, Mark prayed.

CHAPTER 22:

Kathy was deeply worried before she heard the explosion. The teller's computer screens shook, cups filled with pens were knocked over and fell to the floor, sending pens rolling in all directions. She didn't know what to do other than join the other tellers in abject panic. Evidently, her cover had not been blown. She had watched in horror as the towering fake security guard had gone lumbering down the hallway towards the vault, gun at the ready as he went.

She was huddled with the other tellers underneath their counter. Some were praying, others were cursing. Some sat numbly waiting for anything to happen. But when the explosion came, that's when the shit really hit the fan. The tellers broke cover and ran out of the bank as fast as their limbs would carry them, as if the building itself was going to collapse. It did not collapse, but Kathy found herself in a strangely deserted lobby. The tellers had abandoned ship and everyone else in the bank had gone running off towards the vault. She was in a quagmire. What was she supposed to do? This had not been discussed in their meeting last night. They had not covered contingency plans at all. Gabriel had spoken as if it was impossible for them to fail. That had clearly been wrong.

* * *

Mark was thrown to the floor by the force of the explosion. He felt all of the breath leave his body, and he feared that he had a concussion. He lay on his back on the steel floor and looked up. It was steel doors as far as the eye could see, except # 23756 – that one was ripped to shreds and Mark couldn't imagine how lucky he was that none of them had actually hit him – he could have been killed. Gabriel was somewhere vaguely to his left, trying to get up, cursing at something that had gone wrong. Mark wasn't sure. His head was fuzzy. But as he looked up, he noticed something. There was something floating down towards him. It looked like an old dishrag, or a piece of a towel torn from a corner, but that's not what it was. It was floating above the smoke and destruction as if by divine intervention. And it slowly made its way down, down, down until it came to rest over the top of Mark's utterly bewildered face.

* * *

The professor was far from idle during this whole event. After a while he realized that his role as police lookout had run its course. It happened right about the time he heard the second explosion and got out of the car to run to the edge of the parking garage. He was parked on the third floor and he looked down and saw that a massive hole had been blown in the side of the bank, and there were some figures lying on the ground. If he wasn't mistaken, and he couldn't afford to be...that was Mark lying there. He sprinted back to the van and threw it into gear. The tires squealed as he made his way out of the parking garage at very unsafe speeds. At one point on the way down he was on two wheels. But he had to be quick. He had listened to the police scanner and knew it wouldn't be long before the whole area was swamped with police. And he didn't want to spend the rest of his life in a Swiss prison.

"Can you hear me?" he screamed into his headset. There was a lot of interference on the other end, but a voice came through. It was very scratchy, but it was Gabriel's.

"Yes."

"I'm bringing the van around. Get in."

That was all he said.

* * *

Kathy made a decision. She went the way the Luc had gone and found herself in a very long and dimly lit hallway. Most of the lights were blown out but she thought she saw the large fake security guard at the end of the hallway. There were several dead bodies of bank employees on the floor and she stepped over them without looking at their faces. She just couldn't. What had they done? She found Luc. He was lying on his back in the doorway and his head was at an unnatural angle to his neck. He was certainly dead. She saw that Gabriel was leaning over Mark, shaking him, yelling at him.

"Let's go!" he was saying over and over again. Mark got up and saw Kathy who came running towards him to support him. She spoke to him but he clearly couldn't hear her.

"Get him to the van," Gabriel yelled, pointing at the gaping hole in the wall. Kathy did her best, supporting Mark, to get him out through hole out of the bank and into the van. She looked back over her shoulder and saw Gabriel leaning over the spot where Mark had been, and gently scoop something up. He pulled a plastic bag from his pocket and unfurled it. He carefully folded the rag from the floor and put it in the bag. It wasn't until she got Mark strapped in a seat in the van that she realized what it had been that Gabriel was picking up.

"Where's Mizrahi?" the professor said as Kathy was putting on Mark's seatbelt. But she didn't have to answer as at that moment the man in question flung the passenger's seat open and slammed it shut.

"Go," he said.

Gabriel gave the professor driving instructions and the sounds of sirens were both real and imagined to them, the further out of the city they got.

CHAPTER 23:

They drove late into the night, going deeper and deeper into the Swiss countryside. It wasn't until nearly 4 am that Gabriel instructed the professor to pull off the highway and onto a dirt road. The car leaving the highway was enough to wake up the sleeping Mark, who was doing much better. He could still only hear on one ear, but his headache had gone away and Kathy's latent fears about him having a concussion had gone away. He sat up in his seat and inclined it to a sitting position.

"So everything went according to plan right?" he said. Nobody laughed. "Admittedly not very funny," he said. "Where are we?"

"At our destination," Gabriel said.

Automatic floodlights came on as they approached their "destination" and they could see that they were approaching a ranch-style house with an attached barn. There was an old Peugeot with rusted hubcaps in front of the barn, and a fox darted around the corner back into the shadows as they approached. The professor parked the van in front of the barn, next to the Peugeot and took the key out of the ignition. They all remained in their seats. Gabriel took a deep breath.

"Everyone pick a room and get some sleep. We'll talk more in the morning. I think we're all a bit frazzled. Alright?"

There was no opposition to this idea and they all got out. Gabriel (of course) had a key to the house and opened the door. But the long day they had all had did not end there. When Gabriel opened the door to the kitchen the light came on and there was a man sitting at the kitchen table. There was a Tumbler of Scotch in front of him, and the butt of an expensive Gurkha in the ashtray and the scent of cigar smoke lay heavy in the air. He had a gun trained on Gabriel's chest.

"Good morning, Gabriel," he said.
It was Reginald Astair.
"Lovely morning, isn't it? You look tired." Gabriel didn't respond. "Well okay then, you don't want to talk. I can understand that. But now – first give me your gun, then the shroud."

"Let me do all the work for you, eh?" Gabriel said as he removed the Desert Eagle Mk VII from his shoulder holster.

"Easy there Mizrahi. Nice and steady."

Gabriel set the gun on the floor.

"Now kick it over nice and slow."

Gabriel slid the gun across the wooden floor with his foot. Reginald Astair leaned down and picked up the gun; he slid it into his waistband and resumed his seat.

"My dear friends," he said to the professor, Kathy, and Mark. "Don't look so concerned. Come in. Come in. Gabriel, why don't you take a seat – here." He motioned with his gun for Gabriel to sit across the kitchen table from him.

"Now," he said. "The shroud. You did get it, didn't you?"

"Kill me," Gabriel said.

Reginald Astair laughed a dry, humorless laugh.

"If that's really what you want I can oblige, but remember your words to our friend here. If you can't have it, nobody can." Gabriel shot him an irritated look. "Oh yes. I heard that. If I kill you it'll be mine anyway. Wouldn't you rather live to hate me a little longer? Of course I'm not going to let it be an even playing field from here on out. You will take some losses. I can't deny that. But I'm not a monster. And now the shroud, please."

Mark watched as Gabriel withdrew a Ziploc bag from the messenger bag he had been carrying and slid it across the table. Reginald Astair barely gave it a second glance before he motioned for Mark, who still standing in the doorway, to come over to him. Reginald handed him the clear bag and told him that there was a safe in the bedroom at the end of the hall.

"Choose any combination you like," he said. "Why don't you two go with him? In the meantime Gabriel and I have some business to talk."

None of them objected, or would have known how to object. They had no words left after the day they had been through. They walked the hallway of the empty country house as they were told. The allure of searching for historical artifacts had dissipated for the time being. They were nothing but terrified.

CHAPTER 24:

The three of them spent the rest of the night in the bedroom with the safe. They had heard no loud noises from the kitchen and they could only assume that no more violence had been done that day than they had already witnessed.

Reginald Astair was cheerfully drinking coffee in the kitchen in the morning when they woke up, and he made no mention of Gabriel Mizrahi. One of the men who had abducted Mark from his apartment in DC was standing in front of the stove and frying some bacon.

"You all look famished," Reginald said. "Let's have a nice breakfast and discuss some things."

"I'm just wondering..." Mark said.

"How long I've known where you were?" he completed Mark's sentence for him.

"Well," Kathy said, pouring herself a cup of coffee from the pot, "Yeah. I think that's pretty much what we were thinking."

The professor sat down at the kitchen table silently.

"Entirely fair question. Entirely fair," Reginald said. He signaled to his servant to bring him some bacon and eggs and thanked him as he heaped a healthy amount of each onto his plate. "And I will do my best to answer it, as well as fill you in on what I have been up to while you were under the thumb of Gabriel Mizrahi. First of all...I have known your whereabouts for several days and yes I knew what you were doing at the bank. I attempted to intervene there, but I did not... as I assume you did not expect what happened at the bank to be quite so...dramatic. There was a rather large congestion caused by police vehicles and even I cannot influence everything. Is that satisfactory?"

In truth, it was not satisfactory, but there wasn't much else they could have hoped for.

"So...the shroud?" Kathy said.

"Was never part of my plan, but I'm certainly not going to give it up now that I have it. However, for me it is only of secondary importance. It isn't the grail. I'm not of the same mind Gabriel Mizrahi is with all that nonsense about trinity and the crown of thorns. But it is certainly an interesting historical object. I assume the two of you would still like to examine it in order to confirm if it is the real deal?"

Mark and Kathy nodded.

"If we can," Mark said.

"Of course. And then we'll get back to the task at hand."

"The grail," the professor said quietly in a dejected tone. "The grail."

"Yes, Dr. LeTrec. The grail," Reginald said. "Do you have anything else to add?"

"Only that I can help examine the shroud."

"How is that?" Mark said, his interest piqued.

The professor reached deep into the pockets of his khaki slacks which he had been wearing for longer than he cared to think about. He pulled out a keyring and shook his keys.

"I've still got a key to the lab at Sorbonne. When I was Mark's professor at the University of Chicago I was granted rights to use the Sorbonne's laboratories. I assume when they fired me, they forgot to reclaim the keys, so we can still do the carbon dating there. As long as it's not during regular working hours. I'm assuming that you," he looked at Reginald, "Don't have access to carbon dating equipment?"

"I don't. That's excellent Dr. LeTrec." Reginald Astair put a hand on the professor's arm, who looked entirely uncomfortable about the situation. "We'll go to Paris just as soon as we can. And from there we go straight to Cyprus."

The question on everyone's mind was what had happened to Gabriel. Mark and Kathy could not help but notice that Reginald had been referring to him in present tense, so they assumed he was still alive, but they did not envy him for whatever he was going through at that point in time.

"We'll talk more on the plane," Reginald said, getting up from the table. "I'm sure the three of you have a lot to talk about without this old man yammering on." He put his hands on Mark's shoulders. "I'm glad to have you three back."

The three of them sat around the kitchen table at the cottage, seemingly rescued and safe, but not feeling much better about their situation. If Mark was to be honest with himself, he would have had to admit that he felt worse, less safe, than he did the day before. But he didn't say that. He sipped his coffee and sat in silence.

CHAPTER 25:

Reginald's plane was as luxurious as ever, and the airport was only a short motorcycle ride away. They found out that morning that Gabriel was a serious collector of motorcycles. He must have been a real enthusiast. When Reginald pulled open one of the massive barn doors, they found his collection. The door opened with a loud creaking noise, and dust flew up in billowing clouds. But when the dust cleared, they saw ten or more vintage motorcycles. This time, they each had a motorcycle to themselves. Mark rode a vintage 1949 Indian Scout, and rode far ahead of everyone else.

He let the wind blow through his hair; he went without a helmet. He tried to clear his head and think about his priorities. His life had recently taken a whole lot of dramatic twists and turns. Some had been good. It was hard to believe that he and Kathy were a couple, and at this point there was no other way to describe it. Only a few weeks before he had been scared to talk to her at all except within the confines of the hole. But a few weeks before he had also never witnessed death. The skull of the bank employee was still shattering inside Mark's head: over and over again. The cool Swiss country air was a salve to his physical, mental, and emotional wounds.

"Which one do you want to take?" Kathy had said when they were looking at the motorcycles. She was looking at 1937 Harley Davidson WLDR with a sleek red fuel tank and amazingly well kept chrome handlebars. She sat on the seat to try it out. "This one is comfy."

"I'm thinking about this one," Mark said, eyeing the one he would eventually choose.

"Well, it doesn't look big enough for both of us," she said, giving him a frown.

"Well," he said. "Yeah."

He was unable to adequately put into words how he felt, that he needed some time alone to think, to put things in perspective. But Kathy could understand just from looking at him what was going on. She didn't push the issue, but gave Mark a swift kiss on the cheek and hopped on her WLDR. She kicked it into gear and let the engine roar. She clipped her helmet on under her chin and puttered out of the barn, leaving Mark to himself.

When they got to the plane, Mark was more himself, and even the professor, who was always down around Reginald, seemed to be in a better mood. They were, each of them, allowing themselves to be excited again about the journey they were on. The mood on the plane was cheery and Reginald Astair had several bottles of French Champagne opened.

"To celebrate the fellowship being back together again. May we have nothing but success," he said.

They all clinked their glasses and allowed the alcohol to course through their veins and make them feel more relaxed. They were only planning on staying in Paris as long as it took to do the carbon dating on the alleged shroud. The professor was the only one who had ever done the procedure before.

"The actual process will only take a few hours. But we'll have to prepare the sample, and we won't have the benefit of a lab for that. I'd say I need two or three days," he said when Reginald asked him about the procedure.

"And how accurate is it?"

"Well, I'm not theist, but I assume we're looking for this to be around two thousand years old, and if that's the case, very accurate. The process hits a ceiling at about 30,000 years while beyond 10,000 years the accuracy is less consistent." He took another large sip of champagne. "The only way to really foolproof the process is to divide the sample into pieces and do the test more than one time. But I imagine you don't want that to happen."

"How big do the pieces have to be?" Reginald said.

Mark leaned in to the conversation.

"Quite small," he said.

"Miniscule," Kathy added. "It would really be the soundest scientific decision. I mean...I know we'd be potentially cutting the burial shroud of Christ, but for a reason, and it's microscopic. No one would be able to tell."

"Cut it up!" Reginald shouted and tossed his champagne glass into the air. It crashed against the ceiling of the plane and Reginald laughed uproariously. He rang a bell and a man came to sweep up the glass. Reginald always seemed to be making messes and having somebody there to sweep it under the rug for him. But everyone on the plane was too drunk to care. They were headed to the city of love to carbon date the burial shroud of Christ.

CHAPTER 26:

They found themselves once again in the city of love, but they were arriving somewhat worse for wear and considerably more jaded than they had been before, short though the time between visits had been. Mark was no longer mesmerized by the people and atmosphere of Paris as he had once been. He still found it to be a breathtakingly beautiful place, but he now saw everyone around him as a potential kidnapper or killer, or someone he might be forced to kill, and he didn't like this newfound consciousness. He had heard in a college lecture once that human beings developed higher levels of intelligence once they learned to feel empathy. Mark felt like he was having a similar experience. What was it about being a human being that had become so difficult? There were thousands of animals that could do things that human beings could never dream of doing, but they didn't have empathy. Mark cursed his empathy and its ability to destroy his perception of Paris.

He looked around at all of the happy Parisians walking arm in arm, and he saw a couple sharing a baguette under a tree. What was more Paris than that? Nothing, and yet he could not find it within himself to smile.

Kathy put her arm through his and his mind came to rest.

"What're you thinking about?" she said, looking up at him in a way that brought his existential crisis to a shrieking halt.

"Just that I'm glad you're here," he said. Kathy gave him a slight frown, but turned it into a smile. She knew he wasn't giving everything up, but she was happy to find out that she could make him forget whatever it was that was on his mind.

"Well," she said. "You should be."

She gave him a kiss on the cheek and they walked through the park. They had some down time on their first day in Paris because they couldn't do anything with the shroud until late at night, and as long as they allowed Reginald's bodyguards to casually follow them they were free to do whatever they wanted. They stopped on a bridge and looked down at a free flowing stream and saw yellow and orange leaves flowing by in small clumps. They linked hands and looked into the stream, feeling calm. Other couples walked by and to the casual observer, Mark and Kathy looked no different than these couples. Just another couple of foreigners in town to borrow a bit of the Parisians special sauce, that little bit of romance that can only be found in their fair city with charming bistros and parks with bridges, and leaves that always seem to be yellow and swirling in the streets in the best way possible, never getting stuck in gutters, but flying by idyllic couples as an omen of good times to be found just around the bend.

* * *

The professor wasn't spending his time walking in the park with a lover. By lunchtime he was lurking outside of the Sorbonne laboratory. He wanted to wait until the archaeological researchers went to lunch (a very long lunch, because it was Paris) and see if his key still worked. If his key didn't work it was going to stall their plan and they'd have to break in. After the bank situation, breaking in was the last thing he wanted to have to do. So he sat on his bench across the street and ate an apple. More ominously, he drank wine from a paper bag. He felt he deserved it after everything they had been through. His hat was pulled over his face like a caricature of someone trying not to be recognized. He was only a few blocks from where Kathy and Mark were enjoying their romantic walk but he didn't know that.

At a quarter past eleven he saw three men leave the laboratory and he slowly got up. He left the hat pulled over his face and walked across the street. He walked along the building a few times before he felt reasonably certain that he was in the clear. He sidled up to the door and got the key out of his pocket. It was sweaty and slippery. It had been in his pocket all day and his nervous hand had rested on it and picked it up periodically. Before he had time to put the key in the lock, the door to the laboratory opened and nearly hit the professor in the forehead. He stumbled backwards.

"Terribly sorry," the voice from behind the door said. "Didn't expect anybody to be hanging so nearby."

The professor tried to pull his hat back onto his head and slink away, but a firm hand fell on his shoulder.

"Claude is that you?" the voice said. The professor was forced to turn in surprise.

"Hello, Remy."

"It is you!"

* * *

Reginald Astair was thinking about the past. The shroud was in its package on a table in his hotel room, but it was not the only item of his thoughts. It was the catalyst for a much greater stream of thoughts...thoughts of a much younger man. Himself, of course. He paced his hotel room and wondered what had happened to that ambitious, but principled young man. The ambition had survived into old age. Many years before, Reginald Astair had been a graduate theology student, sharing an off-campus apartment with his best friend, Gabriel Mizrahi. They had a shared passion: the grail. It was a bit of a running joke among the other students, the two of them, huddled in their apartment, dreaming of being treasure hunters. But they didn't let it bother them. They wouldn't let others come in between them; they would do that well enough for themselves.

It happened one summer when neither of them was taking any classes. They were about halfway through their graduate program, but they were not the type of students to simply let the summer melt away into a haze of margaritas, beaches, and pleather back seats. They spent copious amounts of time at the library, leafing through their favorite volumes, and studying the text of new books the library had gotten in. It was on one of these days, when Reginald was lying in bed nursing a nasty summer cold that Gabriel had come bursting into his bedroom with a book in his hands and an unreadable look in his eyes.

"Reginald, this changes everything," he said, eyes flashing.

"Unless that book is an instant cure for the common cold I'm not particularly interested." He pulled the covers over his head and told his friend to go away. Gabriel pulled them down and shoved a book in his friend's face.

"Look at this," he said.

The book was titled: The Other Trinity.

"What about it?"

Gabriel then spoke so fast that he had to start over multiple times so that Reginald could keep up with what he was saying. He was talking excitedly and with a passion that dwarfed anything Reginald had ever seen.

"Are there others?" Reginald said.

"What?" Gabriel said, annoyed at his friend's question.

"Well what does he cite? Does anyone else believe it? Or is it just a theory?"

"You don't understand," Gabriel said, getting off his friend's bed, taking his book with him. "I'll explain it again when you're well."

He left his friend's bedroom, but their friendship would never be the same again. Neither one could make the other understand. They were still both committed to the idea of the grail, but the theories put forth in The Other Trinity would never let Gabriel Mizrahi go. For months the two roommates argued about it, and Reginald refused to put it on the same plane of importance as other grail theories on the basis that it was not supported by anything else.

"But it makes sense," Gabriel said for at least the tenth time.

"But so do any number of things after the fact. Remember the thing about The Wizard of Oz we learned in economics? About it being all about the gold standard?"

"Yeah."

"Made sense, but it had nothing to do with the author's intention. Someone went in after the fact and connected dots with their own lines. It's much easier to do after the fact. And that theory made perfect sense, except that anyone acquainted with the history of L. Frank Baum and the Oz series knew it immediately for what it was: nonsense."

Their friendship never recovered.

Reginald Astair paced his hotel room and stopped. He looked at the shroud and thought about what he had done to his former friend. True, he could have done worse, but it still weighed heavy on him. His life had come full circle.

CHAPTER 27:

Claude and Remy were having coffee three blocks from the laboratory under the pretense that the professor had been there to visit him in the first place. They both knew it was utter nonsense, but no one had breached the subject. The professor was sharing somewhat vague details about being an art dealer and Remy was listening politely. The professor stopped speaking when the door to the cafe slammed shut from a sudden gust of wind and the way he jumped was not missed by his former colleague. Remy looked at him intensely.

"Are you alright?"

"Me?" the professor said. "Fine, fine."

"Claude," Remy said putting his hand across the small, round table with coffee grounds strewn across it on the professor's wrist. "I was always on your side you know. You were a great professor. The students loved you. I tried to get you another chance. It looks like you've got it together now, so what are you doing here? Why were you trying to get into the lab?"

The professor flinched again. He had been that obvious? Of course he had been. He tried to push the bottle of wine that he had left on the bench out of his mind, as if doing so would prevent his friend from realizing he had been wrong.

"I was just..." he hesitated.

"Locks were changed two years ago," Remy said, taking a sip of his café auf lait. "Nothing to do with you of course. Just standard stuff." He put his coffee back down.

The professor's hand stopped fingering the sweaty key in his pocket. He looked up at his former colleague.

"I need in the lab."

Remy took another sip. "Now we're getting somewhere."

* * *

Mark and Kathy had slowly made their way back towards the hotel. They didn't go back right away, but to a cafe only a few blocks away. They didn't want to go to their room. Mark was sipping his water in silence when Kathy pulled something out of her pocket and slid it across the table. It was the note from the Watters' book.

"Have you thought about this at all?" she said. Mark was surprised that she had saved it. It hadn't crossed his mind at all.

"Been a little busy being blown up and robbing banks," he said.

A few heads in the cafe turned their way.

"I wouldn't go shouting that from the rooftops," she said through her teeth. She pushed the note further across the table. "At least think about it," she said. "While we've got some down time. Relatively speaking."

Mark took the note wordlessly and put it in his pocket.

"I'll think about it," he said.

They finally made their way back to their hotel room after another hour spent pleasantly at the cafe. It is wonderfully easy to pretend the world is a simple place with the aroma of coffee in the nostrils and the gentle chatter of voices in the ears, blocking sinister memories and anxiety about the future. Mark slid the keycard to their room and noticed that their television was on. He couldn't remember leaving it on. Kathy looked at him. They were both on high alert.

"Probably just the maid," Mark said. He picked up the remote from the bed and was about to turn it off when he realized what was on. It was the news, and it was in French, but the frozen image of the torn-apart bank was hard to miss. Had it really been that bad? The fire raged endlessly in the news loop and rubble lay scattered in the Geneva Street. He had been in shock and hadn't been able to fully appreciate it. He switched the TV off.

"Just the maid," he said.

CHAPTER 28:

Reginald, Kathy, and Mark were sitting on the bench the professor had sat on some twelve hours before. The professor was late and they were getting worried. Reginald was puffing a cigar that had long since gone out, but he didn't seem to have noticed. Mark was playing with a piece of paper in his pocket. Kathy was the only one who seemed to be relaxed, though she was far from it. She was simply the best at hiding her discomfort. She rubbed Mark on the back with the palm of her hand to try and calm him down. He turned his head towards hers and gave her a wry smile. No one wanted to consider why the professor was late. Their only seemed to be a couple options, and none of them were good. There was always the possibility that he was drunk somewhere, and that wasn't good. But even worse was another option: that someone knew what they were doing and had captured him.

But their fears were off base. The professor came strolling up to them a few minutes later, with another man. Reginald Astair stood up, his natural posture of defense.

"Who is this?" he demanded.

The professor raised his hand in a conciliatory gesture.

"Relax Mr. Astair. He is the solution, not a problem."

"Explain," Reginald said.

"My key doesn't work anymore," he said. "But Remy here is the solution."

"If we needed someone," Reginald said. "To help us break in, you should have just told me. One of my men is more than capable of doing it and bringing in common criminals without first consulting me is unwise."

"He's not a criminal." The professor said. "Well not for a few more minutes anyway."

"I should hope not," Remy said, offering his hand to Reginald. "Remy Agee. Associate Professor at the institute of Archaeology." He waved a key in the air. "And I have no need to break into the lab. I have a key."

* * *

Once in the lab, Remy flipped on the lights and asked Reginald for the sample. Reginald handed over the bundle and Remy handed it to Claude. Each of them put on surgical gloves and spread out the shroud on a metal table with a very dim lightbulb hanging above it. Remy withdrew a scalpel from a drawer and carefully cut two tiny samples consisting of a few only millimeter-long threads off the edge of the shroud and put them into two small Petri dishes using a long surgical pincette.

"The painful part is over," he said. He folded the shroud back as it was and nodded to Reginald.

"And now," the professor said. "Hard truth time. The next part is very boring and will take a few days."

"I understand," Remy said, "that you have some travel plans to Cyprus. I would recommend you go ahead and start that trip. You don't have to wait for the results here – you'd only be in the way."

Mark couldn't believe Professor Agee was speaking to Reginald Astair, but the man's confidence was fascinating and Mark couldn't but admire the man.

"I can leave you someone to protect you," Reginald said, surprising everyone. "That is, if it is acceptable for you."

"If you consider it necessary, I would appreciate that," Remy said, politely smiling at Reginald.

CHAPTER 29:

The group was about to willingly split up for the first time. They agreed that the professor was to stay in Paris and to meet them in Nicosia in five days' time with the results, be they good or bad. Reginald approved of the plan, because his purpose was solely the grail, as always.

"So where," Kathy said as they boarded Reginald's plane again, "do you suppose Judas went upon arrival in Cyprus?"

"That's where it gets hazy," Mark said, taking his seat. "But there are a few places to start."

"Such as?"

"Turkish controlled Northern Cyprus," Reginald said as boarded his plane. "The Turkish invasion in 1974 after the constitutional breakdown and some bloody fights in the 1960s lead to the split Cyprus and now we have to live with the consequences." Neither Mark nor Kathy took the time to wonder why the answer seemed to come so quickly to the old man.

"One of which," Mark said. "Was the looting of southern, Greek-controlled Cyprus. Museums were hit hard. They were notoriously close to the chest about what they had in their museums, so what they had in their museum storages we don't know. But what we know for certain...and what the public refuses to acknowledge...is that those stolen artifacts are a large part of the reason the country is still split."

"Sounds delightful," Kathy said. "Not dangerous at all."

"Don't worry my dear," Reginald said. "Money talks."

* * *

As it turned out, Claude and Remy were not destined to have an uneventful few days. That first night, after Reginald, Mark, and Kathy had left, they had spent their time preparing the sample and reminiscing about old times; students, faculty meetings, and so on. It had been altogether pleasant, and they had been expecting more or less the same thing when they returned to the lab the next night. But they were in for a surprise. Someone was already in the lab, waiting for them.

"Good evening, gentleman," the man said as Remy flipped on the switch. Claude nearly jumped out of his shoes and the man noticed and laughed mirthlessly. "Please," he indicated two lab stools in front of him. "Have a seat. Let's chat."

The two men took the stools and waited for the stranger to continue.

"My name," he said. "Is Lloyd Rica Niri. And I believe the two of you have some explaining to do. Explain to me why you are testing my shroud, and what exactly you're doing to it."

"Your shroud?" Claude said incredulously.

"That's right. My shroud. Stolen from my safe deposit box. But that's not what I'm upset about. I'm mostly upset to find the two of you here and not the men who stole it. Tell me, where is Mark Lockheed? I fear I may have overestimated him."

"Unlikely," Claude said.

"The fact that he is not here proves you wrong on that front," the man said calmly. "So how goes the carbon dating? You'll find quite soon that it's every bit as old as you hope. But who cares? Nobody but Gabriel Mizrahi. And from what I hear...he's going through a rough patch these days."

"I'm sorry," Remy said hesitantly. "I don't seem to understand what you want from us. Mr. Rica. Is there anything you want us to do?"

"I like this one," Lloyd Rica said. "Cuts right to the point. Yes there's something I'd like the two of you to do for me. Now listen very closely because I do not like to repeat myself."

The two leaned in closely and were able to see the man's shoulder-holstered IWI Jericho 941 MK VII that until now had only vaguely been showing under his jacket.

CHAPTER 30:

The group flew into Greek-controlled Paphos Airport and was met on the ground by some of Reginald's men who always seemed to be one step ahead of them on the trail. Reginald would not share with Kathy or Mark how they were getting to Turkish controlled northern Cyprus. The border was a dangerous place and was not easily crossed by even the most influential of individuals. Therefore they drove to a nearby hotel and had to wait until the morning when Reginald and a bunch of his men lead them through a maze of streets until they arrived at the outskirts of the city.

There a jeep was waiting for them that brought them to the village of Tsakistra, from where they walked a well-worn path that didn't appear to be going anywhere. The village was fading into the background and quickly there was nothing but sparse vegetation alongside the road. The path slowly increased in grade, and Mark found himself wishing he had a motorcycle again. After nearly two hours of hiking, the path evened out. Mark's shirt was soaked through with sweat and he had an extra shirt from his backpack tied around his head. Kathy hadn't spoken in an hour to save breath. Only Reginald smiled. After ten more minutes of walking they reached a solitary well. Kathy couldn't help but wonder what purpose a well could serve this far away from any settlement. Reginald stopped right in front of it.

"Well," he said. "Down we go."

"Excuse me?" Kathy said.

"I think I know what he means," Mark said, starting to understand. "A rebel tunnel."

The well, if it could be called a well at all, was not deep. It was not more than a forty-five foot drop, and when they reached the bottom they could see what they couldn't from the top of the shaft. There was a tunnel that went unmistakably north. Reginald pulled out three headlamps from his bag and gave one to Kathy and Mark, strapping his own around his head.

"Archaeologists shouldn't mind a little tunneling, am I right?" he said. He was practically giddy.

As they walked, Mark explained to Kathy that during the coup d'état 1974, rebels had built tunnels in order to move troops and (allegedly) stolen or looted items. Mark found it grimly appropriate that they were using one of the tunnels that perhaps the grail had already travelled in the not so distance past. The tunnel was stiflingly dark, even with their headlamps, and they had some scares with sudden appearances of bats, but all in all their first few hours were uneventful. They had about ten miles to walk before they would reach the border, and Mark and Kathy could do the math. They would be spending at least a night in the tunnels, possibly more than one. It wasn't something they looked forward to, but they accepted their fate. Five hours into their hike from Tsakistra they were forced to accept the inevitability of a night spent in the narrow, stuffy tunnel.

It was Reginald who ran into the problem first, quite literally. He stumbled over a pile of rubble that their headlamps had been unable to adequately light up and right behind it the tunnel was blocked. The rebel tunnels were more than forty years old, and Mark had already given some thought to the possibility of a collapse. Still, it was a difficult moment. They all sat down at the blockage and were silent for a time.

"We need to rest," Reginald said. "Before we try and make our way through this."

Mark and Kathy had to agree. They were exhausted. After the hike to the "well" and the nearly six miles they had walked underground, they needed a break. They were almost too tired to even be worried about being trapped in an underground tunnel forever. Almost. They sat with their backs to the walls of the tunnel, next to each other, their legs entwined, and Mark shone his light on the note he still had in his pocket. A thought had come to him during their hike and he hadn't been able to shake it. It was plausible, if unlikely.

"I've been thinking," he said. "About the note."

"Yeah?" Kathy said. She looked up. She had been close to nodding off. Reginald snored, propped against the blockage in the tunnel.

"Yeah. I used to know this guy. In school. He was obsessed with anagrams. Always used to say how the cleverest people were those who could anagram."

"He sounds like a nut."

"Well that's just the thing. He got put away. In an asylum. When we were juniors in college."

"What's this got to do with the note?"

"A lot," he said. "Taken one by one the words don't seem to matter."

"But altogether?" she finished for him.

"They're impossible to miss. He was adopted by this incredibly wealthy Swiss family, the Niris. They both died in an auto wreck and left him everything. That was when he started to lose it. He took his anagramming fad to a whole new level. He started to believe that anagrams had some kind of cosmic significance. The last name of his adoptive family anagrams to…"

"Jesus Christ," Kathy finished for him again.

"Yeah," he sighed. "And naturally he latched onto me. He knew about my obsession. Everybody did. He wanted to help me, but he wasn't an archaeologist. He was a mathematician, or he wanted to be. He wasn't any help to me. This was around the time the school was considering kicking him out. They had a counselor talk to him and everything. I mean…it was obvious that he was over the edge. He was stalking me… anagramming everything about my life, trying to connect himself to me somehow."

"And?" Kathy said.

Mark held up the note. "Cordially," he said. "That's the greeting at the end of the note. He didn't omit a signature. It anagrams to Lloyd Rica. That was his name."

Kathy gasped.

CHAPTER 31:

It did not take Claude and Remy long to figure out that they were dealing with someone who was not entirely beholden to facts and figures, despite his multiple references to being a mathematician. He was prone to long bouts of rambling, and he talked a lot about how his fate was entwined with that of Mark Lockheed and of Jesus Christ. None of it made very much sense, and Lloyd Rica's insistence on speaking in a tone of epic gravitas all the time did not help them decide what was important and what wasn't. It came down to this: Lloyd wanted them to arrange a meeting between himself and Mark Lockheed, and the two of them had wordlessly decided that it would be a terrible idea to do so.

"He'll be back in France," Claude said. "We can help arrange something then."

"No. I want you to take me to him," Lloyd Rica said. "I am meant to be with him every step of the way, or the journey will be tainted, incomplete. I am the Christ that he needs with him to find the cup. You can't find the cup without the Christ." This was one of the lines that he often repeated and Claude and Remy had no idea how to deal with such psychobabble. They were archaeologists, not psychiatrists.

"Alright, then," Remy said while Claude looked at him pleadingly. "We'll take you to him. Revel Thou in the morning?" he suggested.

Lloyd grinned at Remy broadly.

"Certainly," he said. "Don't be late."

"We won't."

"Of course you won't. I'll be watching."

After Lloyd Rica had left the lab and their breathing had returned to normal Claude stood up and paced the room.

"What the hell was that babble? How did you get him to leave?"

"Anagrams. Bit of a hobby of mine in high school. Seems to have come in handy. He's off his rocker isn't he?"

"What did you say?"

"We're meeting him at the Louvre at nine o'clock in the morning."

The professor, not as skilled at anagramming, needed a moment to work it out in his head.

"You can't seriously be thinking of meeting him? We'll just have to find another lab."

"Not unless we get more samples. We already started the process, and we don't have the shroud anymore. But no...I don't think we should just play his game. He's dangerous."

"I'd say so," Claude agreed. "He thinks he's Jesus Christ or something."

"He's probably schizophrenic," Remy offered thoughtfully. "They tend to place an undue amount of importance on things that normal people wouldn't. In his case it's anagramming. He thinks that there are no coincidences with anagrams. Because his last name anagrams to INRI, and with your friend Mark he met someone who was looking for the Holy Grail... he saw a cosmic connection. And schizos don't just let these things go. It's a bit like dealing with a religious zealot. You can't talk reason."

"So what do we do?"

"We use his paranoia against him," Remy said, getting off his stool. "But first...you need to get better at anagramming."

CHAPTER 32:

It was slow going. None of them wanted to admit it, but they were moving the smallest rocks first because they were afraid to move the bigger ones. They could have caused another collapse and create their own tomb. Mark stopped to wipe his forehead on his shirt. It was hot and stuffy in the tunnel. Their poor lighting from their headlamps made the work even more difficult.

"Five days," Reginald said. "If we don't come out in five days my men know to come in after us." It was meant to be more comforting than it was, but Kathy nodded at him as if it made her feel better. She felt even worse about the situation after Mark's solving of the mysterious note from the book the night before. If he was right (and she knew he was) then they also had a lunatic stalking them.

They had been digging away at the blocked passage for several hours when Mark stopped and dropped the rock he was carrying.

"Hey, stop," he said to Kathy and Reginald who looked at him as if he was crazy. "Don't move," he whispered. It didn't take long for them to realize why he had said so. They were not alone down there. There was unmistakably the sound of digging and scraping, and it was not coming from them.

"Someone is digging from the other side," Kathy said quietly. Mark nodded. He sat down and put his back to the tunnel wall.

"Sounds like they have shovels," he said. "Shouldn't be too long then."

"That's it?" Reginald said, seemingly to be utterly at a loss. "You've got nothing else to add?" Reginald Astair had a tone of panic about him that was not very becoming, and that Mark and Kathy were unaccustomed to seeing.

"Did you want to turn back?" Mark said, somewhat bitingly.

"No."

"Well... this is what you signed up for," Mark said. "This was always going to be dangerous. All we can do is hope that they're friendly."

"What are the odds of that?" Kathy asked.

"Not good," Mark said. "Not very good at all."

Mark was right about at least one thing. It did not take them very long. It was only another thirty minutes before they could see light in the cracks. The people who were digging towards them had much brighter lights along with their shovels. They were speaking fast in Arabic and their words carried through the small cracks in the rocks alarmingly. Reginald, Mark, and Kathy stood up when it was clear that they would be breaking through at any moment. Mark took Kathy's hand and squeezed it. Reginald sweated through his shirt.

They stepped back as the head of a shovel burst through, followed by a gloved hand, shoving debris out of the way. The shovel hit again, and then a boot, and then a man was able to squeeze through.

He did not seem surprised to see them. He looked them up and down and asked them in unaccented English is they had any weapons on them. Reginald turned over his pistol and Mark and Kathy insisted they had none. The man asked them to put their hands in front of them and he zip-tied them. He didn't do it too roughly; he was gentle enough.

"You are under arrest for attempting to unlawfully enter Northern Cyprus. Do you have any questions?"

They didn't. It was clear to them that these men were not officers of the law, but were also accustomed to tunnel sneakers. The man who had zip-tied them and another lead them through the tunnel the way they had been travelling. The man instructed the others to continue clearing the tunnels. It seemed to Mark that if Northern Cyprus was still maintaining the tunnels they were probably still using them. But what for?

CHAPTER 33:

Claude was irritated. He was not good at anagrams. He had never seen the point. And he wasn't getting much better.

"What's the point of this?" he said for the umpteenth time as he paced the floors of Remy's apartment.

"It's how this guy operates. Clearly he has a lot of money. Enough to make people forget that he's a loon. But you see he can't get past anagrams. They're sacred to him. He has to see them as important. He's hardwired that way. It's really pretty simple. We just craft a few anagrams to lead him astray, enough to buy us some time to finish the carbon dating and get the hell out of here."

"To Cyprus."

"To Cyprus."

"Okay, hit me again."

Claude and Remy practiced through the night and by the time the sun rose over Paris, they had a pretty good idea of what they were going to tell Lloyd Rica.

"It's completely absurd," Claude said as they drank coffee in the morning to stay awake. "It's never going to work." He was going through a bit of a last minute panic.

"You can't think that way. He won't think it's insane. He'll treat it with reverence. You'll see. It'll work."

The professor was going through something that those who make money with words often go through: disbelief. He couldn't believe that some silly combination of letters could lead to real world consequences. But he had to believe it. The man was crazy. The man was rich. And the man had a gun. So he would believe in the power of words, even if he wasn't happy about it.

They left Remy's flat with plenty of time to spare. Their walk to the Louvre was slow, deliberate, and silent. What neither of them knew as they walked with their hands in their pockets and their faces turned down to the Parisian sidewalks, was how little all of their planning and logical thinking would turn out to matter. They had approached their dilemma as scientists are apt to do: logically, critically. And they can hardly be blamed. They were presented with a mad man and they prepared as if for a presidential debate. They did not leave room in their plan for the one thing that should have been expected beyond all others: the unexpected.

They knew something was wrong by ten after nine as they sat on the edge of the fountain in front of the Louvre. Neither of them wanted to admit it until well past a quarter past nine. At that point, they exchanged looks that said it all. They were beginning to understand that their planning wasn't going to help. It was Remy's back that the pistol was jabbed into. He jumped and nearly stood up, but the voice that breathed down his neck told him to only stand up on his command. Claude froze. He was in a better position to make a move, but he didn't have the mental fortitude.

"Now," the voice said. "Slowly stand."

It looked to any casual passerby as if Lloyd Rica and Remy were a couple, walking close, arm in arm, and as if Claude was their third-wheeling friend, unwilling to let them get too far out of his sight. They walked for what seemed like an eternity to the petrified scientists. They found themselves in the eighteenth Arrondissement, where the buildings were gray-scaled and low slung. A third story window across the street broke and a record player shattered on the street. A taxi swerved around it with no squealing of tires; the status quo was not broken. Finally, Lloyd led them into an alley and into a building up a tired set of stairs that groaned under their weight. They went up ahead of him and since they were inside now, he was able wield the gun behind them openly now.

"It's unlocked," he said up the stairs as they reached a grimy door with a small steel reinforced window that was dirty enough to become useless. "Open it. Sit on the floor."

Remy opened the door and the sight that greeted him and Claude was truly horrifying. The apartment had a single bulb hanging down from the ceiling on a power cord. It was swaying, though there was no movement of air in the stale, cramped room. It was a single room and there was no furniture. The walls were covered in pictures of Mark Lockheed. Some of them were in minor scientific journals, the kind that takes work to find. But others were far more alarming in their candid nature. Claude and Remy didn't have time to dwell on the presence of the pictures of Mark, because the rest of the room begged for their attention. Bolted into the floor were corrugated steel loops with heavy iron manacles. They looked like they belonged in the Marshalsea prison in early nineteenth century London, not in twenty-first century Paris. And yet they loomed, and from the scattering of oddly shaped metal objects around the room, the two scientists became keenly aware of what was intended for them. The outlook was not pretty.

They sat on the floor slowly as Lloyd Rica closed the door behind him and rubbed his sleeve on the window in the door as if to clean it. It looked the same when he was finished as before he had started. He rubbed the side of his nose hard enough to draw blood on most people, but he seemed unperturbed.

"Put them on," he said, his voice breaking. The two men he had captured didn't know how difficult this was for him. His confidence was hanging by a thread. "They click when they're locked."

The two men on the floor did nothing.

"Do it!" Lloyd screamed maniacally, and the two men reached for the iron shackles to seal their own fate.

CHAPTER 34:

They walked in single file for a very long time before they were allowed to rest again. By Mark's calculations they were likely to be out of the tunnels by morning. He wasn't even entirely sure that it was nighttime, but it seemed as if it were to him. The man who seemed to be in charge of the operation set a lantern on the ground and everyone sat around it as if it were a campfire.

"So," Mark said. "I'm Mark."

Kathy and Reginald Astair stared at him in disbelief.

"I know," the man said coolly, unzipping his backpack and taking out a piece of jerky. He tore a piece off with his teeth. He tossed the other piece to Mark. Mark brought his ziptied hands to his face and tore off a piece of the dried meat. "Are you waiting for my name?" he said.

"I don't' think we have enough time for that," Mark said, and the man laughed a raspy laugh that echoed in the tunnels.

"I like your attitude, Mr. Lockheed. Very charming. I'll be sure to mention that to my superiors."

"And who are they?"

"The rightful government of Cyprus of course. And there are some other interested parties involved."

"The border patrol, I assume?" Mark said. "Since we've been apprehended illegally crossing the border."

"You believe that is your only crime?" he said, again reaching into his pack. This time he pulled out a folding knife. He flipped it open and it made a satisfying clicking noise. He began to clean out grit from underneath his nails. "I hate it down here," he said. "Disgusting being underground." He grunted as a particularly large piece of grit was dislodged from beneath the nail of his pointer finger.

"I can't imagine what else we've done," Mark said. "We're very curious archaeologists who didn't want to bother with the red tape of international travel. You know how it is."

"I do indeed, Mr. Lockheed," the man said. "Know how it is. And for that reason I know that you are full of shit." He gestured at Reginald Astair. "Your friend is awfully quiet. Why don't you ask him if he's got any ideas?"

The man realized that he had caught Mark off guard and he smiled, pleased with himself.

"So you don't know everything there is to know about your traveling companion then."

"Don't listen to anything he says," Reginald said, and Mark couldn't help but notice how pathetic he sounded. "Cypriots aren't to be trusted under any circumstances."

"Tut tut tut," the man said. "Not a flattering look on you. You should have stayed in DC Astair. Should have stayed in DC. You just can't let it go."

Mark looked at the man in the face, trying to get a read on him. The light from the lantern cast an eerie light that only truly illuminated his lips and chin, leaving the rest of his face in an underground shadow.

"Yes. I know what you're doing here," he said. "Looking for Judas. You're hardly the first. But," he said, cocking his head. "You do deserve some special credit for starting the trend. That paper you wrote sent many people our way. Part of the reason your name isn't very popular in these parts. Not very popular at all."

The man laughed his horrible, hacking laugh again and Kathy leaned up against Mark's arm. She rested her head on his shoulder and she was far away, back in the Swiss countryside, standing next to an idling motorcycle, looking off into the beautiful distance. She was not in the cave as Mark was. He wished that he wasn't.

"I don't believe you," Mark said, unconvincingly.

"Very well," the man said. "But you will soon."

CHAPTER 35:

Remy never forgot the first time he heard a gunshot. In the movies and on television, it's never portrayed as loud enough. That was the thought that pervaded his twelve year old brain more than anything else. Partially because he was unable to emotionally deal with the brain matter that found its way onto the tip of his size seven light-up sneakers, but also because of the sheer surprise at the force of the sound.

His father had taken him out for sorbet like they had so many times before. His mother had died two years back, and it had been hard, but his father was doing the best he could and Remy was an unusually bright boy who could recognize that and appreciate it. One of his father's earliest solutions to having suddenly become a single parent was sugar. He didn't know as much about children as he would have liked, but he knew that they liked sugar. Remy wasn't even particularly fond of sorbet, but he was particularly fond of the idea that his father was trying. So, shortly after his mother had died, the tradition of going to get sorbet on Saturday mornings had been born. They always walked from their flat and took the longest route they could. They walked through the park and took several block detours around crowds of people. Their journey usually took them more than an hour both ways, though it could have been a mere fifteen minutes. It was an exercise in father-son-bonding.

This particular morning it was drizzling, and they didn't make quite as many detours as usual. That isn't to say that they were hurrying, but the rain, paired with the general malaise of monotony that comes with any routine, even one as pleasant as a sorbet-run, put a small dampener on their spirits. Soon, very soon, they would simply be happy to be alive. It happened while Remy's father was waving off the change to the owner of the sorbet stand, who by now was basically a family friend. Remy's father instinctively took his son to the ground and covered him with his body, but it was too late for any sort of protective action. The shot had gone off only a few feet from them, and neither of the men's eardrums would ever be the same. Someone had pointed a gun at a man somewhere behind them in line but he had refused to give up his wallet. He had reached for the gun and it had gone off. At that range, there was very little left of his skull. By the time Remy's father had brought him to the ground, the mugger was a block gone, panting heavily, never to come back for his gun.

Remy stood up as his father had let him go, suddenly aware that the danger had passed. Remy had watched as people around him looked at him and their mouths moved. Nothing was coming out but it looked uncannily like they were trying to talk to him. They pointed and he looked down at his feet. There was something gray and lumpy on his shoes. The man who had stood up for himself was lying a few feet away. In the distance sirens rang out. It was the first noise that made him realize he could hear again.

* * *

Remy never forgot what the sound of a gun going off at close range sounded like. The early trauma had indelibly marked him and as he watched Claude struggle with Lloyd Rica he knew what was going to happen, long before it actually did.

When Lloyd had instructed them to manacle themselves to the floor, Claude had acted as if he was going to do just that, but had grabbed the heavy manacle and thrown it at Lloyd Rica. Luckily, the chain was just long enough for the heavy piece of metal to hit Lloyd in the stomach and catch him off guard. Claude moved with surprising agility and lunged at Lloyd. They struggled for the gun with alarming intensity. Remy was frozen to the spot, his childhood memories clouding his judgment, though his present brain was very much aware that the fate of his life rested in how the struggle that played out in front of him ended up.

The gun went off. It was every bit as loud as Remy remembered and when it was over, Lloyd Rica lay on the floor of the flat and the two scientists waited in silence for the police to arrive and take them away. But minutes passed and nothing happened. No one seemed to have taken any notice of the gunshot. Lloyd Rica's blood spilled on the floor and soaked through Claude's shoes and socks. He threw the gun in the corner in disgust. It skidded across the floor and came to rest near the wall.

"Is he?" Remy said, finally breaking the silence.

"Yeah. He's dead."

They both knew it, but it had to be said. Nobody could lose that much blood and survive. It was impossible.

"What should we do?" Claude said, stating the obvious question which neither of them had an answer to. "Do we turn ourselves in? It was self-defense. He was going to torture us."

"No. Absolutely not. We don't do that."

"Then what?"

"We bury him."

"Are you insane?"

"I'm beginning to wonder, actually."

CHAPTER 36:

The literal light at the end of the tunnel was not a
pleasant sight for Mark, Kathy, and Reginald Astair. As long as
they had remained in the tunnel, the outside, and all the
consequences that came with it were only an illusion, something
that would not become real until it was directly in front of their
eyes. And there it was. The bright Cyprian sunshine, its bright
happiness doing its best to mock them. Their captor took a deep
breath of air as he emerged from the tunnel and put his hands on
his hips.

"Breath the free air, my friends," he said. "Enjoy it for
the moment while you can."

The sights of an actual city were surprising. Though
they had only been in the tunnel for a few days, it seemed a
lifetime. They were not yet aware of it, but they were in Lefka,
just on the other side the border to Northern Cyprus. The city
had little meaning for any of them but Reginald, who had been
there before...

They were put into the back of a sliding-door van with
a siren. The traffic moved out of their way and they traveled
quickly north.

"Where are we going?" Mark ventured to ask. Their
captor from the caves was sitting in the passenger seat, and the
driver was a stranger who stared forward at the road as if his life
depended on it.

"Since I might as well tell you at this point," he said.
"We are going to the prime minister's house. You'll have to be
cleaned up first of course, you're filthy."

"There's no prime minister," Reginald said. "Filthy
rebels don't have official titles."

"Your friend is very rude," the man said. "But I can
assure you with utmost confidence that that is where I am taking
you. I would not lie to you. Prime Minister Kamali is very tired
of Mr. Astair here. Very tired. And you have had the misfortune
of being found with him. For that I am sorry," he said.
"Particularly for you," he said, directing his eyes at Kathy. Mark
could feel her shudder. Their captor smiled and for the first time
they could see his teeth in the daylight. A gold incisor glinted at
them as he turned back to the front of the car. "It's not a long
drive. We'll be there in no time."

The man, as far as Mark could tell, had indeed been honest with them. After an hour they pulled up a deserted road to a wrought iron gate. The driver of the van rolled his window down. He punched in a nine digit code and the gate slowly opened, squeaking on its tracks. There were another several miles to drive up the road before the Prime Minister's house came into view. It was a house with several gables, built in an English style with impressive natural stone walls at the vast sides of the domicile. It looked remarkably out of place, sitting by itself on a barren hill. There were no trees or anything to see for miles around. Mark could see men with guns in black outfits patrolling the grounds. He couldn't imagine why they needed to. They could stand in one spot and see for miles.

"Fun fact for you two," their captor said. "This lovely house was built by your friend here."

Mark and Kathy turned to Reginald. He said nothing and did not deny the claim. It certainly looked remarkably similar to the style of the house that Mark had first been taken to back in DC. That night was an age ago to Mark and everyone involved.

They were let out of the van and their ties were cut. There was nowhere to run anyway. The man snapped his fingers and two of the guards Mark had noticed came up.

"This," he said. "Is sadly where we part from each other."

He took a deep bow and walked off back towards the gate. Mark couldn't imagine that he was going to walk all the way back down. But he didn't have too much time to think about it because he was taken by the arm, not altogether gently and lead towards the house. He noticed that the closer they got, the greener it was. It looked like the owner of the house was building his garden from the walls outward and had only been able to get a hundred feet or so. When the house was directly upon them, there was an abundance of greenery. Mark saw, in the short time he was afforded: orange trees, tulips, white oleanders, along with any number of plant species that Mark was unfamiliar with. He was far from an expert in botany.

After entering the massive house Mark and Kathy were led to a bedroom suite and asked to make themselves presentable. The door clicked behind them and was locked. Somehow, they knew that their new friends were stationed just outside the door in the hallway.

"So," Kathy said. "Sweet digs."

And they were indeed. The suite was palatial. The floors were well-buffed marble, and the ceilings were thirty feet high. The bed was in the center of the circular room, canopied in a white, gauzy veil.

Mark threw open the closet doors and found what could have been a bedroom all to itself. There were plenty of clothing options for both of them and he turned around to tell Kathy and saw her figure disappearing under the canopy of the bed. The canopy still rippled slightly. He walked to the bed and parted the curtain. Kathy was on the bed, shed of all her clothes, and beckoned to him.

"What do we have to lose?" she said. Mark let the curtain fall behind him and joined her on the bed.

They were as loud as it pleased them to be, letting the guards outside their door know that they were still in there, and they were very much alive.

CHAPTER 37:

Gabriel Mizrahi was a patient man. He bided his time in Santander . At least his old friend had been kind enough to place him in a town that was so beautiful. His truly loyal associates would find him. It might take them some time, but they would find him. He spent his days working on the boats, constantly accompanied by his two unnamed guardians. The men that Gabriel worked with had many rumors and theories as to who the men Gabriel lived with were.

It was a beautiful seaside villa that he shared with the two men. The other men who worked on the boats tried to get something out of Gabriel but he always simply insisted that they were his "bodyguards" which wasn't entirely untrue. He never elaborated beyond that or provided any context for why a boatman would need a bodyguard, much less two. They could never get anything out of him. He did his work and kept to himself. He seemed to be an experienced seaman, but he would never tell them where else he had worked in the past. He was really the greatest gift that the small-town men had ever received. The months that Gabriel Mizrahi was around, they always had something to talk about over their boxed lunches.

Santander was mostly a tourist town. The fishing industry was really the only thing that was still organic about the place. That's not to say that it wasn't beautiful, but one could only hear so many tourists gush about the boulevards and the beaches before they became tainted and ordinary. The locals kept mostly to themselves and their own haunts that were seldom visited by tourists, save the most intrepid and adventurous ones that strayed off the beaten path.

Gabriel had little problem settling into the local routine of sticking to oneself. Some of the men at the docks said they saw him occasionally down at the city center. He always bought books and carried them back in his arms to the shore. They figured he must have had plenty of time to read since he never left the villa except to get books and go to work. What was his deal? They never did figure it out. One morning, he simply didn't show up to work, and he never would again. They continued to gossip about him for a few weeks after his disappearance, but eventually Gabriel Mizrahi would slip from the collectively sleepy consciousness of the locals of Santander, Spain. It was as if he had never been there at all.

That morning that he didn't show up to work he had fully intended to. But he arrived in the breakfast nook of the villa to find his two "bodyguards" slumped over their coffees, dead. He checked their pulses carefully. They were indeed gone. He was pleased, but not alarmed. He went about his morning business in the same manner he always did. He stirred his instant coffee into the steaming water and sat down in the window seat of the nook. They'd be by any minute now. He watched as a tourist learned to parasail and got knocked down by a big wave. He chuckled to himself. He heard the front door of the villa open and he took a generous sip of his coffee. He rubbed his hands on his sailor's overalls. He supposed he'd need to change. They'd have clothes for him.

"Hello," he said as his associate came into the kitchen. "Very nice work."

"Mr. Mizrahi," the man said, bowing deeply. "We are sorry it took us so long to find you."

Gabriel put his hand up to quiet the man and his other associate who now made his way into the room.

"I am thankful for your service. Both of you. I knew you were faithful and that you would find me. The length of time is of no consequence. Santander is lovely, though a bit nosy."

He laughed and his men laughed with him, slightly irritated at their boss's good humor.

"If Reginald were smart he would have killed me, no?" he said, drinking the final sips of his coffee. His men were silent. "It's alright," he said. "It's true. But he couldn't bring himself to do it. His emotions got the better of him. But now, let us move on. You do know where we must go now?"

"Back to Paris?" one of his men said tentatively.

Gabriel clapped his hands enthusiastically.

"Yes, my friend. Yes. You have both done really well."

CHAPTER 38:

Remy's father had not been pleased with his son's insistence on going to the man's funeral. They had read in the paper that the service would be held on Saturday morning, their sorbet time. Remy, who even at his young age, had a firm grasp of metaphorical resonance, felt it was appropriate. But his father was concerned that his son wanted to go at all.

"But we don't even know him," his father said.

"We were there. We have to. Didn't you see in the paper that he was a widower? No family at all. It's very sad."

"Yes, but we are not his family."

"Papa," Remy said. "Were you in the hospital room when Maman passed?"

"Yes," his father said, choking up a little. "I was."

"And me and you and Maman were there when grandma died. Your family is who is there when you go. We were there with him. We should go to the service, Papa."

Remy's father couldn't believe the words coming out of his son's mouth, but he had to admit that they made sense even if in a strange way. In the end, he would agree to go, and it would even make him feel better about the whole situation.

* * *

Remy was not making the same kind of progress Claude. Claude could not understand why Remy was so calm, and why he was insistent on burying Lloyd Rica.

"He tried to kill us. And we don't even know him."

"That's not the point. It's about decency. He clearly had issues of his own. He deserves a burial as much as anyone else," Remy said.

"No one even saw us come in. We can just leave. We have work to do. We have to keep working on the carbon dating."

"I can't even believe you're thinking about that right now," Remy said.

"I need a drink."

There was a profound silence. Claude regretted his words, but they had been true.

"Look," he said. "You aren't thinking practically. Logistically, how would we even do that?"

He was surprised to find out that Remy had in fact already considered logistics. And he listened for the next ten minutes as Remy laid out what he believed to be the best way for them to go about properly disposing of Lloyd Rica's body. Claude listened in guilty silence and was slowly won over by the precision and logic in his old friend's plan.

"Fine," he finally said. "We'll do it."

As he was not covered in blood, Remy was the one who left the apartment first, when darkness had descended over Paris. His first order of business, as he had been rather flustered earlier, was to discover where exactly in Paris they were and how far away they were from a potential final resting spot for their would-be torturer. That didn't take him too long, and he made his way to a twenty four hour convenience store shortly thereafter. He purchased: two tins of peaches, (they were both starving and would need their strength) two large coffees, and a set of men's clothing. He bought Claude a pair of jeans, socks, and sandals, as they were the only type of shoes sold, and also a heavy winter coat. His final purchase was two plain black hats. He made his way back to the flat in no great hurry, carrying his odd assortment of items with the pride that comes with doing the right thing, of which he was quite certain.

When he returned, his friend was pacing the floor, tracking blood as he walked. Remy didn't draw attention to this fact, as Claude seemed blissfully unaware.

"Jesus Christ you took your sweet time," he said as Remy closed the door behind him. "Let's just do it."

Remy tossed Claude a can of peaches and held up the coffees to the light.

"Eat. You're frantic. You need to eat."

They ate in silence and when they were finished, Claude changed clothes in the dim light of the still-swaying overhead bulb. Inexplicably, there was a large blue tarp in one dark corner of the apartment. Remy had been the first to notice it, and he thanked heavens for not having to buy a tarp on top of everything else. They went about wrapping the body of Lloyd Rica in the tarp. When that was finished, they waited for the dead of night. They had settled on four am as the best time to do it. It was a long time to wait.

When the time finally came, they put on their most officious airs and carried the body in the tarp down the rickety stairs they had been forced up at gunpoint. The closest cemetery was a mere two blocks away. The streets were completely empty until they were less than a hundred yards from the cemetery, when they met a police officer. Remy tipped his plain black hat to the officer.

"Morning, officer," he said. The policeman wrinkled his nose at the tarp.

"That what I think it is?" he asked.

"Sure is, sir. Real tragedy this one."

The officer walked with them along the sidewalk as they could not simply set the body down.

"Very sad," Remy continued. "Gunned down at a sorbet stand is what they tell us."

The officer shook his head and muttered something about the depravity of the modern world.

"Couldn't do what you two do," he said. "Couldn't do it."

And with that, he was gone. He continued on his patrol and the two men made their way through the gates of the cemetery. Claude could not believe what had just happened.

They took the body to the back of the cemetery and set it down gently. They walked, free of their burden, to the shack that held everything they would need. It was closer to the street, but they were more confident in their cover now. Remy looked behind him at the quiet street before he pulled the weapon out of his coat pocket. He brought the butt of the gun smashing down on the old lock on the door and it went to the ground with a soft tinkling noise. Everything was going according to plan.

Until they heard a groan.

CHAPTER 39:

It didn't take Mark long to get showered and changed into a tux. He found himself unsurprised that the massive closet had a tux that felt as if it had been tailored for him. If there was anything he had learned of recent, it was to accept things as they came to him. He sprawled back on the canopied bed and called into the bathroom for Kathy.

"Almost ready now?"

"Putting my earrings in," she called back.

Mark couldn't help but chuckle. It was like they were getting ready to go to their friend's wedding, like they were in a suite of their own choosing and purchasing, and not one that they had been thrust into after being kidnapped. They were becoming experts at making the best of a situation.

When she finally came out of the bathroom, Kathy looked ravishing. She was wearing a strapless emerald green ball gown, and she had her hair pinned to an elegant chignon. She was sans makeup; it was the one thing that had not been waiting for them in the suite, but she looked stunning nonetheless. Her earrings were understated chandeliers, nothing too fancy, but they worked perfectly. Mark gave her a slow clap.

"Oh stop," she said. "Let's go see the newest rich man who is going to boss us around."

"Does seem to be a theme doesn't it?" Mark laughed and knocked lightly on the door of their room. There was a shuffling of feet and then it was pulled open by one of their guards.

"Right this way," he said.

* * *

Reginald Astair had spent his time in his equally grand suite, yet in a much less pleasant state. He sat slumped up against the door, listening for the guards to give up something important, since he had little else to do. He knew he was supposed to shower and change, and he couldn't deny what he smelled like after a few days in the tunnel, but he couldn't bring himself to do it. This was what happened to grail seekers. The grail didn't want to be found. No matter how hard he tried, there was always someone else there to stop him. He was having a crisis. He had dedicated his life to finding the grail, and it had done nothing but mocking him and biting him in the ass. He was allowing himself a moment to wallow in self-pity over his utter defeat. But still...in the back of his mind it was there. There was the image of the grail in his hands, drinking from the cup, the gritty water going down smooth. He could not deny that either. It was as real as anything to him and it was not an image he could shake. Through his constants defeats, it was what kept him going, and as he sat slumped against the door of his suite it came to him again. He stood up and walked to the bathroom. He needed to look presentable.

* * *

Kathy and Mark found themselves in a grand hall, being led over a red carpet towards a man sitting in what could only be described as a throne. Yet the man, who sat on the raised platform, so that his knees were at eye level with them, did not look like a king, but like a commoner - a prime minister. He was wearing a crisp, gray suit and vest and had a closely trimmed beard. He wore round, metal-rimmed glasses. The only thing flashy about him was the gold watch around his wrist which he casually checked as he got up and walked towards the couple.

"Welcome, welcome," he said. "Though I must admit that it took you longer to dress than I would have imagined."

He offered his hand to a bewildered Mark and shook it vigorously. He took Kathy's hand and kissed it before giving it back to her. He looked into her eyes and gave her a million watt smile. He spun around quickly and clapped his hands. A group of men appeared out of nowhere and carried in a dining table and chairs.

"Very good, very good," he said, and gestured for Mark and Kathy to join him at the table. "Please, please," he said. He had the noticeable linguistic habit of repeating words, but it came across in a pleasing manner. He unbuttoned his suit jacket and threw it over the back of his chair theatrically. He clapped his hands again and more men appeared with steaming dishes. "Lovely, Lupe, lovely, thank you, thank you," he said, taking the proffered cloth napkin and folding it in his lap. He beamed across the table at Kathy and Mark who were doing their best to appear at ease, though it must have been obvious that they weren't.

The meal turned out to be lobster with a seemingly infinite variety of sides. Prime Minister Kamali ate with uncommon gusto and any idea that the food might be poisoned went straight out the window. Mark and Kathy were actually quite famished after spending so much time in the tunnels eating jerky, and their appetites showed it.

"Beats Moubry's tunnel jerky, doesn't it?" their host said, laughing to himself. "I'll never understand that man. Never understand," he said. "Very strange, very strange. I bet he walked back to the gate after he dropped you off, didn't he?" He could see from the looks on his guests' faces that he had guessed correctly. "Not surprised, not surprised. He's an odd cookie."

That comment from their host, had they been more at ease, would have elicited a laugh, as goldentooth was undoubtedly a very strange man. When the meal was over and it was time to get to business, the prime minister wiped his mouth with his napkin.

"I can tell that the two of you are worried. You've no need to be. Moubry has told me that you are not to blame. Your companion, Reginald, ah Reginald...that is not quite the case. You two have simply made an employment mistake. Forgiven, quite forgiven I assure you."

They nodded and thanked him profusely. He put up his hand to silence them.

"But there is something I'd like to talk to you about. I know what you are doing...as I can easily explain to you, as you are far from the first to sneak into my country with that man with the very same goal. It is...partially your fault, and I'm tempted to hold it against you, but I find your writing in the essay in question so charming that it's hard to do so. What I want is for you to continue...but for me."

Mark took a moment to wipe his mouth with his napkin, though he didn't need to. He was giving himself some time to fully gather his thoughts before he responded. It was tricky territory and he didn't want to offend anyone.

"I'd be lying if I said we hadn't heard that pitch before," Mark said, and Kathy put her hand over her mouth and nearly laughed.

"Mizrahi?" the Prime Minister said. "Those two really need to get a room don't they?" He laughed to himself. "I can assure you that my pitch is a little bit different."

"How's that?" Kathy said.

"I'd like you to destroy it."

Kathy dropped her wineglass and it shattered on the marble floor, her wine pooling at her feet like blood.

CHAPTER 40:

The groan came from inside the cemetery shed. Remy pushed the door open before his nerves became too frayed to serve him properly. And they were rewarded with the most amusing they had seen all night. The groan had come from the groundskeeper, who had grown too drunk and managed to lock himself in the shed. He lay on a bag of mulch and had a bottle of cheap Armagnac between his legs. The two men stared at him and the groundskeeper stared back. There was no understanding in his eyes.

"We've got your shift covered," Claude said, getting control of himself. "You can go home."

"Porbly need ta," he slurred, trying to stand. Remy hunched down and helped the man up. He wobbled a little once he was on his feet, but he didn't look like he was going to fall down.

"Do you live far?" Remy asked. All they received in return was a violent shaking of the head.

"'Sanks," he said, and tried to tip his hat. Yet all he did was knocking his hat on the ground. Claude picked it up for him and placed it back on his head. He noticed that it was a plain black hat very much like their own and he couldn't fathom how lucky they had been.

"Get home safely," Claude said.

Claude and Remy watched in disbelief with their hands on their hips as the groundskeeper weaved down the street and around the corner. Luck really was on their side that night. The two men were too afraid to discuss their good luck, so they retrieved the shovels they were looking for and headed to the back of the cemetery to do their unsavory work. Remy thought to himself that Shakespeare must never have actually dug a grave, or his depictions of the event would have been less quippy. Digging a grave long and deep enough for an actual human being was more difficult than either of them had imagined and it was sweaty work. Once in a while they had to stop, exhausted, and lean on their shovels. They spoke little and Remy lead his mind wander to the past.

* * *

Remy and his father had attended the funeral of the man they had witnessed being gunned down. Remy's father had spent the morning scouring newspaper stands to try and find any information pertaining to the criminal investigation, but it seemed that the police had given up entirely on finding the man. That was the reality of police work; it was mostly failure. He read about the man whose funeral they were going, and was sad. The man, as his son had told him, didn't have anybody in the world. He had been a university professor (and when Remy many years later took over a professorship it was not lost on his aging father) and had lead a mostly solitary life after his wife had passed at a young age. He never remarried, but by all accounts he had been a lively and friendly man, happy to discuss anything with students and faculty alike. His field of study had been philosophy and Remy's father wondered what he would have made of his manner of death. He surely would have had an apt syllogism for the moment of his own death, but Remy's father didn't know it.

Remy and his father had been the only two people at the man's funeral other than those who were there by contractual obligation. It was unbelievable to both Remy and his father that none of the man's students or coworkers had shown up. Philosophy must have been a very cruel field of study is all that either father or son could think about. As a result, the two of them spent the morning at the funeral in the most solemn and earnest display of true mourning that had ever been felt for a total stranger. As the priest said his words, tears went down Remy's face for the first time since his mother had died. Was this all that life had in store?

* * *

"I know someone buried in this cemetery," Remy told Claude, breaking the silence that had lasted for several minutes.

"What?" his friend said.

"Over there," Remy pointed, leaning on his shovel. He had realized which cemetery it was when he had set out hours earlier from the dead man's flat. He had given some consideration to looking for a different cemetery, but it seemed to be an untenable idea. "At least I think that's where it is. Hold on." Remy climbed out of the hole. It was big enough now that it took some effort. They had made some very good, silent progress. Claude watched him walk across the cemetery and felt compelled to follow him. And so he did. When Remy had stopped he was staring at a grave that looked neglected. There were some weeds growing on it and unlike most of the graves around it, there were no wilting flowers that had been lovingly placed. Claude watched as Remy got on his hands and knees and started pulling out weeds with violent force. He threw the weeds across the cemetery in every direction with a righteous sort of anger. When he was finished, he sat on his knees, panting, staring at the gravestone. It was an old, faded stone; cheap, probably paid for by one of those charities that bought headstones for people without any estate.

"Who is he?" Claude asked.

"Nobody," Remy said. "Nobody. Just an old university man like us."

Remy stood up and put his hand on Claude's shoulder.

"Let's go finish."

Claude noticed that there were tears rolling over Remy's cheeks and he felt he understood, to a small extent, why Remy had been so set on burying the man who had intended to torture them into revealing Mark Lockheed's location. He didn't fully understand, and he never would, but he could live with that.

They did their work quickly from that point on. When they were finished they patted down the area as best they could. They felt satisfied that they had done right by the mentally disturbed man. They carried the shovels back to the shed where they had found the drunken groundskeeper. They put the shovels back in their place in silence and closed the doors.

They did not look back over their shoulders as they walked away down the street. Remy suggested that they go to the lab. They needed to check on the carbon dating progress. Claude nodded in agreement. He had almost forgotten the reason he had reconnected with his former coworker. It was a long walk but neither of them complained. They needed the walk and it was a cool, pleasant night. But when they reached the lab they could see that something was wrong. They were walking at the edge of the park across the street and could see that there were two people standing in front of the laboratory door. And they were not two ordinary people.

Their uniforms gave them away. They were police officers.

CHAPTER 41:

Gabriel Mizrahi was on a roll. The trip back to Paris had been a rejuvenating one for him and he felt alive again. He had not realized how much he had been in hibernation mode while in his forced exile in Spain. But he was back and his vision was as clear as ever. He paced the old, cracked, wooden floors of one of the many flats he owned in Paris and explained his plan to his men. There were more of them now; some of them had come out of the cracks when news had gotten around that he had returned. He even found out that a few of them had continued working as if he had never been gone. They explained that they had faith and had assumed he would return. He clapped these men on the back heartily and listened raptly to what they told him. They had kept an eye on what had been going on in Paris and told him that the professor and another man were up to something in a research lab not very far from where they were currently sitting.

The rest of the plan was relatively simple to figure out. It was not difficult for a man like Gabriel to acquire disguises that would pass a superficial inspection.

"Tonight," Gabriel said to his gathered men. "Is when we make our move. Why waste any time at all? You have all surpassed any expectations I could have for you. You are truly excellent companions."

Gabriel allowed his men to bask in his praise for a few moments before moving on to more explicit details of the plan. There was a small amount of dirty work to be done in order to attain the uniforms necessary. There was also the matter of who would be doing the actual work. He decided that two would have to be the number. He had never seen more than two police officers on patrol together and any more than that would draw an undue amount of suspicion that was entirely unnecessary. The rest of the team would be in charge of less exciting but equally important tasks like surveillance and preparation. Gabriel left it up to his men who would accompany him into the laboratory where the two men had been working. They had earned at least that much.

"I'm going to take a nap," he told them before they had a chance to really get their ire up at each other. "So please let your discussion be civil. We'll all be up very late tonight." He smiled at them and went into the bedroom, closing the door behind him. As he lay on his back and stared at the dusty ceiling fan he continued to smile. Things were on track again and he was pleased. He had no idea if he'd even be able to go to sleep, though he certainly needed to. He was simply too excited. Had it really been less than twenty four hours since he had been forced to listen to the banal chatter of the Spanish boatmen about their wives, children, and gardens? He pitied the men he had met more than they could have ever imagined. They had no adventure in their lives. They did not have a driving purpose like he did. All they had to care about was their jobs and their very, very small lives. His life was grand and he intended for it to become grander any day now. He could hardly contain his excitement.

* * *

Gabriel Mizrahi dreamed of his life as a younger man. In his dream he was back in college and on the couch with Reginald. They were watching university television. They were some of the only students who ever actually watched the low-budget fare run by students. But today that proclivity was paying off. Their eyes were glued to the screen.

"Have you heard about this?" Gabriel said to Reginald, his eyes not leaving the small, fuzzy television screen. The snow falling over the student reporter's face did little to the reverent mood for either of the two young students.

"No. Nothing."

The student reporter was explaining that their university was going to be the recipient of a very large grant given for a very specific purpose. They were to receive the equipment necessary to perform Carbon 14 dating. They were speechless. They had spent countless hours together discussing the grail and how if (they found it) they could be sure they had the right item. They were very much against sharing the credit with another already established grail seeker, and the solution had dropped directly into their lap.

Many years later, the sleeping Gabriel Mizrahi felt very much the same way – as if the solution to all his problems had simply fallen into his lap.

* * *

The two "police officers" didn't know that they were being watched, or that their presence was being entirely misinterpreted. It would be impossible for them to have known, but the entire premise of wearing disguises was based on the idea that they would be seen, even in the absolute dead of night. They didn't bother to hide what they were doing because they were dressed as police officers. Anyone who saw them would assume they were on official police business.

They forced the door to the lab open and went inside.

CHAPTER 42:

Back in the fancy suite, Mark and Kathy tried to figure out when it had gone so wrong. Everything had seemed to be going so well. The dinner had been delicious and mostly jovial in nature. It hadn't been until after he had sprung on them what he wanted from them that they had found themselves in their current predicament.

"He can't keep us here forever, can he?" Kathy said, sitting with her back to the bed frame.

"Well," Mark said. "I hate to play Debbie Downer here, but who exactly knows we're here? It's not like there's going to be some kind of international outrage, and the marines are going to be deployed to save us in a raid. I think we're stuck here."

"What should we do, Mark?"

"There's really only one choice isn't there?"

* * *

Mark and Kathy were unaware that their host had not been entirely honest about waiting for them to arrive for dinner. He knew they would be awhile, to spite him if nothing else. He had not simply been waiting for them in the grand hall. He had paid a visit to Reginald Astair's room.

Reginald came out of the steaming bathroom in a bathrobe, to find Prime Minister Kamali sipping Zivania, a typical Cypriot pomace brandy, from a crystal glass and leaning casually against a bookcase. Salman Rushdie's The Satanic Verses shouted in its loud red font over the shoulder of the powerful man. Reginald toweled his head; he wasn't surprised to see the man.

"Prime Minister. Your manners are lacking. I didn't hear a knock."

Prime Minister Kamali laughed and swirled his drink in his palm.

"Very funny, very funny, Reginald," he said. "But you are the last person who should be lecturing about manners, as you don't have any. How many times have you illegally entered my country?"

"I see no country," Reginald said. "Just a very rich man who launders money and sells guns to crooks."

There was a very small crack in the Prime Minister's smile, but he hid it well.

"Forget it," Reginald continued. "They won't do it. Take my word for it. Don't even bother."

"Oh I know," Kamali said. "I know, I know. Professional ethics and all that. But they'll find it for me."

"Under the pretense of agreement?"

"Obviously."

"I wouldn't be so sure," Reginald said.

"Oh, Reggie, Reggie, you're so unconvincing. You're living proof. They won't be able to resist. It's too late now. They're seekers and seekers don't stop. You of all people should know that. You knew I'd probably get you again, but you came anyway. They're the same as you now."

Reginald clenched and unclenched his fists.

"Why are you here Giorkis? Just to gloat?"

"Reginald you insult me. You know I don't gloat. I've come to offer a deal."

"Our goals that are so far apart I can't imagine what we could bargain on."

"Maybe they're not so far apart as you might think," the Prime Minister said.

Reginald Astair listened as Prime Minister Kamali laid out his plan for him. The more he listened, the more he was able to get on board.

* * *

Kathy and Mark reached an inevitable conclusion. They would tell the Prime Minister that they would help him find the grail in order to destroy it. Obviously, destroying it was not in their plan, and they had to assume that he would know that too. They would have to play the game very carefully, but there was little else they could do. Kathy put Mark's arm over her shoulders and they sat together with their backs to the bed, breathing in deeply in unison.

CHAPTER 43:

Claude and Remy simultaneously broke out in panic. What had happened? They had been so careful. No one had seen them go into the apartment with Lloyd Rica, or at least they didn't think anyone had seen them. But those had been police officers going into the lab. The lab that only they had used over the past few days. They were in the middle of what the university called "research vacation" when most of the scientists on campus took vacation. The officers had to have been looking for them.

They looped back into the park and stopped about where Mark and Kathy had stood together very recently, on top of a small romantic wooden-slatted bridge.

"Are you panicking right now? Because I am panicking," Claude said. "Should we turn ourselves in now? I mean it can't add to our offense that we buried him right? That was just respect for the dead. It doesn't change the fact that it was self-defense. Right? Right?"

"Well," Remy said. "I think it makes it look worse actually. It makes it seem less believable, like we were trying to cover something up. I don't think they'd buy the respect for the dead thing. Even you didn't really buy that at first."

Remy was thinking with a slightly clearer head, as he had not been the one to actually pull the trigger. True, he was still intimately involved and certainly wasn't off the hook, but he didn't have the same amount of guilt hanging over him that his friend did. He put his hands on Claude's shoulders and shook him lightly.

"It's gonna be alright. We'll just have to tell our friends that we were unable to complete our experiment. We can say that the university caught us and banned us from the lab. It's perfectly believable."

"It is, isn't it?" Claude said, his breathing slowing a little. "And the police can't have our names."

"Of course not. What we need to do now is remain calm and head to Cyprus. We'll catch up with them and act like none of this ever happened. Because it didn't."

* * *

The two men, back at Remy's apartment, packed hastily. The first leg of their trip was to be on a train. Neither of them wanted to deal with airport security. They did not honestly think that their faces were going to be plastered on posters all over town or that their passports had been blacklisted, but there was still a paranoia present that kept them from going to Roissy - Charles de Gaulle Airport. They nodded at each other as they left the apartment and they were very quiet on the walk to the train station. They each carried only backpacks. They weren't silent out of fear, but out of a sense of calm determination. They would get to Cyprus. Nothing had ever happened in the last 24 hours.

The train station was crowded though it was still very early in the morning. The two men couldn't help looking over their respective shoulders every once in a while. Remy adjusted the straps on his backpack as a man who looked very much like his father got on the TGV, the French bullet train. This was not their train and that was not his father. He knew these things.

Claude was tapping his foot when the commotion started. A man flew by the bench they were sitting on and he had a bag clutched to his chest. He pushed people out of his way and a woman hit the ground hard. The coffee cup she had been carrying fell with a plopping noise and steam rose from the brown puddle that spread out from her splayed body. Claude could only watch as Remy got up and began running. What was he doing? Was he insane?

Remy was chasing down the mugger without thinking. Claude could not believe his eyes. They were trying to keep a low profile and there went his friend, flying after a criminal in a crowded train station, drawing a huge amount of attention. Next to run by were two police officers. They were not the officers from the previous night. Of course they weren't. He had to shake his head as if to get the stupid thoughts out. That would make no sense. They were young looking officers; they usually were in the train station or places like that. It wasn't an assignment anyone wanted. They huffed and puffed after the mugger and Remy.

Claude stood up to see if he could get a better look, but thought better of it and sat back down. But he couldn't help himself. He stood up and jogged after the mugger and Remy and the officers. He only made it a few columns down when he noticed that their train had arrived. He came to a skidding halt.

Passengers were filing off the train. People like him were lining up to get on the train. Where was Remy? Out of habit, Claude looked at his wrist, though he hadn't worn a watch in years. He nervously looked around. The conductor came over the intercom and said something incomprehensible. Claude did what he had to do: he boarded the train.

CHAPTER 44:

Gabriel Mizrahi could hardly believe his eyes. He had been inside of the laboratory for less than ten minutes, five of which he had spent trying to find a light switch, and he already had a huge breakthrough.

All those years ago, back in college, he and Reginald had been the first students on the waiting list to learn how to use the carbon dating equipment. Gabriel had not forgotten anything. Within a few minutes of being inside the laboratory, he was aware that whatever had been tested, and he was pretty certain he knew what that was, was a couple thousand years old. He could hardly contain his excitement. He danced around the laboratory and grabbed his man's hands.

"Do you realize what this means?" Gabriel said. The man nodded. "We're going to Cyprus, my friend. We're going to Cyprus."

Gabriel did not like Cyprus. He had never much cared for the climate, the people, or the landscape. But at that moment, it was the only place he could even consider wanting to be. Paris was a gutter to him compared to Cyprus. Cyprus was where at least two of the items of the "other trinity" were. He knew that and it made him happier than anything in his life had ever made him before. No woman had ever come close to making him feel how he felt at that moment in that dimly lit laboratory dressed as a police officer.

A mere few hundred yards away Claude and Remy were having a moment of crisis in the park. They were having the exact opposite experience of the Israeli "police officer". They existed at different ends of the emotional spectrum, but their emotions all came from the same place; from the same very old object that was very lost and very much sought by many men who called themselves "seekers" of this object, as if they had a right to find it at all.

CHAPTER 45:

The latest phase of the quest was unlike any of the preceding ones. Its basic components remained the same, but the scale had become grander. There was no denying the Prime Minister Kamali, whatever his flaws, knew how to travel in style. The number of people that accompanied Mark, Kathy, and the Prime Minister was somewhere near fifty. They were riding on horses, walking undisturbed to accomplish their mission. From a distance they looked simply like a long cloud of kicked-up dust. The word "caravan" came to Mark's mind, though he sat on the back of a horse and not a camel. He rode next to the prime minister himself. They were heading into the Kyrenia Mountains that stretched along the northern coast of Cyprus.

"I know that Reginald has probably told you that someone in my country is holding the grail as a result of looting. I will not deny that looting took place." The Prime Minister said. "But I can assure you that if we have the grail I am not aware of it. It is nothing but a burden to me. I have other things to worry about and yet I spend half of my time beating self-proclaimed archeologists away from my borders that are on journeys just like yours."

Mark and Kathy had decided not to ask the Prime Minister what exactly had happened to Reginald Astair. The better decision seemed to be not to know at all.

Mark was not a fan of the two men who rode in front of him and the prime minister. One of them had looked over his shoulder at them as Kamali had been speaking. The two men were robed entirely in black, and their faces were covered by masks. They were, Mark assumed, the Prime Minister's personal bodyguards.

"But you," Kamali continued. "You know better, don't you? Why don't you tell me why we are heading for the region of Kyrenia?"

"There is a legend that speaks of a different type of night journey," Mark said, obliging the Prime Minister. "The night journey of Koranic legend wherein the prophet Muhammad ascends to heaven after traveling to the furthest mosque where he leads other prophets in prayer is not the story we are chasing. As I mention in my paper...there is some evidence to indicate that some Saudi scholars of the time were at the very least...aware of the theory of Judas's flight."

"So he went looking for the grail?" Kathy said.

"And your friend here thinks he found it," The Prime Minister said. "In the mountains of Kyrenia... not at the furthest mosque."

"Well," Mark said. "There's no sense in holding back. That is the theory. He intended to destroy it."

"But he couldn't do it," Kathy said, finishing Mark's thought.

"Exactly. He was a man with reverence for history," Mark said. "Legend has it that though he never wanted the cup to be found... so that his new religion could flourish... yet, he could not destroy it. So he hid it deep within the mountains."

"I will complete his work," Kamali said. "He should have destroyed it when he had his chance, but he went soft at the last moment. The same will not happen to me."

The Prime Minister's further assurances that he would destroy the grail hung like a dark cloud over the party, and they rode in silence for a long period of time. When the silence was finally broken, it was only by Kathy and Mark reminiscing quietly to each other, and wondering what their co-workers back in "the hole" were doing while they were riding horses into the north Cyprian mountains. The image of their underappreciated co-workers, toiling in obscurity in the windowless room where the United States government sends archaeologists to rot like the specimens they study had a surprisingly calming effect. Mark and Kathy each had to privately admit that part of them...those parts that didn't thrive on jet setting and adventure...those parts missed the bad coffee and the cringe-worthy political incorrectness of underpaid government employees, and even the insane traffic of their hometown of Washington, DC.

Mark used his eyes to bore holes in the backs of the black-cloaked security guards for the prime minister and thought about all the trouble he and Kathy had gotten into. They had no clear plan going forward.

CHAPTER 46:

Remy realized his mistake much later than his old friend Claude LeTrec, otherwise known as the professor. He didn't realize the incredible stupidity of what he had done until he was talking with the two pimply-faced police officers who had caught up with him and the victim, but not the perpetrator. Remy hadn't caught him either, but he almost had.

When he had reached the stairs that lead back to the streets of Paris he had jumped over a woman who was leaning down to sweep up some spilled popcorn and landed three steps from the top. He surprised himself with his own agility. As he reached the top step he could see the perpetrator just disappearing around a corner. He looked over his shoulder, down the steps, and saw the pitiful face of the woman who had been robbed, her skin red and blotchy, huffing and puffing to keep up. Remy took off again after the man. Some kind citizens saw what was happening and cleared the way for Remy as he chased after the man. A few even cheered. One man threw his coffee at the thief and his shriek of pain could be heard. Remy was closing in on him.

But he tripped on a crack in the sidewalk and the ground came up quickly to meet Remy's face. By the time he was conscious enough to be on his knees, the police and the woman were there, and the thief was long gone. His nose was bleeding and he staunched the blood flow with the sleeve of his shirt. He realized that he still had his backpack on and it all came rushing back to him in an instant. He wasn't a man who wore backpacks often. He had a roller suitcase. But they had both been wearing them; him and the professor. Shit, he thought to himself, what was I thinking? There was no need to be a hero and now the officers were asking if he could go back to the station with them and give a statement, maybe describe the man to a sketch artist if he could. He had gotten the best look at him after all.

"I don't want to miss my train. Not trying to be rude, but it is important."

"Well," one of the officers said. "Which train was it?"

He told them and the officers and the lady informed him that it was already gone. It had left while he was chasing the thief. Of course it had; it had been nearly time when he had run after the man. He couldn't believe his own stupidity. Had Claude boarded the train without him?

"He has really done enough," the woman said to the policemen, putting her hand on Remy's arm. "Thank you."

"I wish I hadn't tripped," Remy said, offering a wry smile.

"Really, Monsieur... it will only take a few minutes," one of the officers said.

"Sure," Remy said. "I'll have to catch another train anyway."

* * *

The professor was equally upset - he had boarded the train. He could have waited for his friend and they could have boarded the next train together. But he had panicked and had to board.

He was lost in his thoughts, which is why it took him so long to realize that the man sitting across from him on the train was smiling at him. It wasn't the friendly sort of smile that travelers often give each other when their eyes incidentally meet, or even a smile of genuine happiness. It was a mirthless smile and the man who owned it could hardly believe his own luck. Oh yes, things were looking up.

"Pleasure to see you again, Dr. LeTrec," the man said across the aisle. The woman sitting next to Claude could see that the two knew each other and moved down to the row to allow them to chat more openly. When the woman's considerable girth had moved out of the way, the professor could see the unmistakable smiling face of Gabriel Mizrahi.

"I think we have a lot to discuss," Gabriel said. "Shall I get us a private compartment?"

Claude nodded meekly. There was no getting off at the next stop and going back for Remy now. His friend would be alright – he was a smart man.

CHAPTER 47:

The Prime Minister was in his tent. It was really more like a mobile bedroom than a tent. There were four men and four mules that were on the journey exclusively to carry it. It had a plush chair, a reading lamp, a coffee table, among other creature comforts that the Prime Minister felt he should not have to live without. He was sitting in his chair, reading by the light of his lamp, when the flaps to his tent opened and one of his black-robed bodyguards came in.

"My... colleague... would like to speak to you. I told him—"

The Prime Minister put his hand up.

"You did rightly. I'm very tired and will be retiring shortly. Tell him that I will be happy to speak with him later and that for now he should be more focused on the job at hand."

"Yes, Sir," the man said, and turned to leave.

"And Ibrahim?"

"Yes, Prime Minister?"

"Keep an eye on him."

Prime Minister Kamali went back to his book as if nothing had happened and he had not been intruded on. He put his finger to the page in order to follow a particularly interesting bit of text.

Twenty yards away, Mark sat with Kathy, poking a weak fire with a stick. It was cold. It had been scorching during their ride in the day, but after the sunset the temperature had dropped dramatically. They shared a blanket around their shoulders and held each other closely for warmth.

"What do you suppose that's all about?" Kathy said, nodding her head towards the Prime Minister's tent. One of his body guards stood outside the tent, while the other went inside to talk to him. The one outside the tent looked impatient and was shuffling his feet.

"Nothing good," Mark said, rubbing his hands together.

"Have you thought about it at all?" Kathy said. "How we're going to stop him from doing it?"

"It's just about all I've thought about. But honestly... I'm not sure we should."

There was a deep silence between the two of them, and Kathy weighed her words carefully.

"What do you mean you're not sure we should?"

"Well," Mark said, shifting the blanket so they could see each other's faces better. "Is it worth our lives? I have a professional duty as an archaeologist to make sure that the cup is preserved. It's of historical significance. It's thousands of years old. But Kathy... I don't believe it's divine. I'm not Reginald or Gabriel. It's just a cup. Do you want to potentially give up your life for a professional obligation? What if we had a different job?"

"We have to try," Kathy said quietly. "We have to."

Their conversation faded as the night closed in around them and sleep became more important than any moral dilemma.

They awoke in the morning to find bustle all around them. They seemed to be the last people in the caravan who had still been sleeping. Mark and Kathy rubbed the sleep out of their eyes as the Prime Minister, already decked out in all of his riding gear came up to them with two steaming mugs.

"Coffee for my archaeologists?" he said cheerily. Even though they disagreed with him profoundly, they had to admit him a generally charming man.

They stood up to stretch and gratefully accepted the proffered mugs. They watched as some members of their caravan packed bags and loaded up mules and horses. There were shouts crying out in the morning air, orders being given, arguments being had. There was a bustle of activity in the otherwise quiet foothills. The Prime Minister could see Mark's eyes roaming the activity.

"We're paring down the support. Sadly my tent will be among the first things to go."

"Roughing it eh?" Mark said. "They're going back?"

"Not everyone," he said. "Essential personnel will stay on." He did not elaborate as to what exactly that meant. "And a little further on we'll pare down further. Eventually it will just be us. You can't take a caravan into the mountains. Doesn't work that way, I'm afraid."

"No," Mark said. "I suppose not."

The Prime Minister left them to prepare for the morning. He was almost skipping he was so giddy. Mark turned to say something to Kathy, but she was gone.

* * *

Kathy had slipped away while the Prime Minister had been talking to Mark. Her coffee was still on the blanket next to where she had been sitting, throwing steam into the air. She disappeared in the bustle and deployed the only asset that really matters when trying to get something done: confidence. She walked among the men and acted as if she was supposed to be there. She was checking saddlebags and she did it as officiously as possible. She went from mule to mule and nodded at the men as she did. One of the first saddlebags she came across one that had an Ouija board in it, and as strange as it seemed, she knew what to do. She took it out and carried it with her.

It took her several minutes before she found what she was looking for. She looked into the saddlebag and the morning sun glinted off the muzzle. She took the Sarsilmaz 357 revolver out gingerly and grabbed some extra rounds while she was at it. She took the top of the box of the Ouija board and set the revolver and the rounds inside. She carried the box under her arm and headed back to where Mark was. Mark saw her from a distance and gave her a funny look. She was looking at Mark and wasn't looking where she was going. She accidentally bumped into one of the Prime Minister's bodyguards. He shoved her away and she staggered a little.

"Watch where you're going," he said, his voice scratchy. She regained her balance as a strong hand steadied her. She looked to see Prime Minister Kamali standing beside her.

"Apologies," he said. "He has no manners, but good at his job."

Kathy held on to the Ouija board tightly.

"Thank you," she said tersely. She began to walk away.

"And Kathy?" he said as she walked away. She looked back over her shoulder.

"Let's play that game you've got some time. I love games." His eyes were trained on the box she held under her arm. She nodded and walked quickly back to where Mark was standing.

CHAPTER 48:

Remy left the police station and tried his friend's cell phone number several times and it went straight to voicemail every time. He had a decision to make. He could return to his life. He could go on vacation. Now that the panic was over, he was seeing more clearly that he didn't have to go to Cyprus if he didn't want to. But he had to face one fact that had become very clear to him: he did want to go to Cyprus. He wanted to help find the grail. It wasn't his singular passion, but he was an archaeologist and he felt that he had a duty to his friend and fellow scientist.

Outside the station he hailed a cab and got in.

"Charles de Gaulle," he said, and the taxi sped off towards its destination. He wasn't going to miss out on any of the action.

* * *

A few hundred miles away, on a train speeding rapidly towards Bern, and then Milan, the professor was filling Gabriel Mizrahi in on what had happened since the bank heist. Gabriel was genuinely interested in some parts, and at other parts pretended like he didn't know the information already. It was very clear to him that by some incredible force of unlikelihood, they had seen him going into the lab, but he felt that the professor being scared was only to his benefit.

"So I can't tell them for sure if it was old enough to be the shroud. But I have my own thoughts on the matter," he said, steepling his hands and tapping his thumbs on his chin.

Gabriel leaned forward as if eager to hear the professor's professional opinion. He in fact, already knew that the shroud was old enough, and the samples that had been tested were in his bag between his feet at that very moment.

"Do tell," he said.

"I've handled artifacts from that time period before," the professor said. "Of, course it could be a very clever fake... but why make a fake and then stick it in a bank vault? Pretty stupid move if you ask me."

"Why indeed," Gabriel said. He paused for a moment and stroked his chin. "May I call you Claude?" he said.

The professor was irritated at the name because he heard it so little. His ex-wife had always called him Claude; she entirely eschewed the usage of platitudes like "honey" or "sweetie." He was always Claude to her and she was always Karen. His own name had become a kind of talisman that belonged to his now broken relationship.

"Sure," he said. "Why the hell not."

"You don't like me very much," Gabriel said calmly. "And I can understand that. But there's something you also need to understand. I assume that you intend to find your friends. There are only a few places where they could possibly be. I've been to Northern Cyprus before and I can tell you that the leadership is not too kind to grail-seekers... partially because of your former student. Apparently grail-seekers are diverting precious military resources from more important endeavors like bombing the southern end of the country. But this isn't about politics. No... it's more personal than that. Prime Minister Kamali... he hates us. All grail-seekers. I don't know why, but I know it's not because we're cluttering up his country. It's deeper than that. He hides it behind smiles and suits, but he is dangerous. If he has captured your friends, and I assume he has – they are in trouble."

It was a lot of information for the professor to take in at once and he was still reeling from hearing his name spoken by the Israeli.

"And?"

"And you need me. I need you too, but you need me more. We can't just blunder into the country like I'm sure they did. Reginald thinks he's smart and he thinks his money will protect him. But I'm willing to bet it didn't."

"So what do we do now?"

"I've got an idea," Gabriel said.

He reached into his bag and pulled out a flyer for an event taking place in Iskele. The flyer read "NetCon: An Event with Internet Celebrities". The professor turned the flyer over in his hands and gave Gabriel a pained look.

"You think they'll let us walk into the country because you have tickets to some dork convention?"

Gabriel laughed softly.

"You misunderstand me, Claude. We are not going to be guests. We are going to be internet celebrities. If there is one thing that is indelibly true everywhere in the world it is this... celebrities get special treatment."

The professor grasped what Gabriel was suggesting and did not doubt his network's ability to make it happen. For the first time in a while he smiled too.

CHAPTER 49:

It was getting to be tougher going and it was not unnoticed by the remaining members of the prime ministerial caravan. The foothills were slowly becoming steeper and the walking was being done mostly in a gloomy silence. Mark and Kathy wondered to themselves when the caravan would be pared down again, as well as where exactly they were supposed to go once they got into the mountains. Mark's theory had ended in the foothills of the mountains. He had never found any evidence, even of the circumstantial variety, that he felt lead to a point more specific than that. Though he believed it... he knew that his theory about the grail didn't stand on very firm ground. He was a scientist, but this wasn't exactly a scientific endeavor. He was firmly on his father's playing ground of fantasy and religion, but somehow... he knew he was right. What he didn't know was whether or not he was about to waste a whole lot of time breathlessly wandering around the mountains of Northern Cyprus, egged on by a slightly crazy Turk, looking for something that may not be destined to be found.

The image of them searching fruitlessly in the mountains brought to Mark's mind a time in his childhood when his father had posed a Lewis Carroll riddle to him.

"Why is a raven like a writing desk?" he had repeated back to his father from the edge of his bed. He tugged on his pajama sleeves. He was growing too fast and none of his clothes fit quite right.

"That's the riddle," his grinning father had said. "But I can't tell you the answer. That's something you have to figure out for yourself."

And it hadn't taken long for the young boy to give up and ask his father for the answer, but it had taken a long time for him to accept it.

"There is no answer," his father had said. "It was never designed to have one. It's nonsensical."

He had not been a happy camper. He had devoted a great deal of personal time that could have been spent in his treehouse, to trying to solve this riddle that apparently didn't have an answer. He had not realized his father's wisdom as a child, and he often found himself wishing he was still alive so that he could tell him that he understood now.

He had never understood it better than he did while he walked up an increasingly steep grade with the caravan. Life had a plethora of riddles that were likely to never be solved, and he was smack-dab in the middle of one.

The silence of their walking was broken by scuffling. A fight had broken out, and just as if it was high school lunch time, everyone stopped what they were doing; the entire progress of the caravan was halted. The two men had hit the dusty ground with their hands at each other's throats. Everyone was surprised to see that it was the Prime Minister's two bodyguards, those of the black robes and hooded faces. Giorkis Kamali stood frozen in place and his right arm was out from his body like he was going to do or say something, but ultimately couldn't.

The men wrestled and writhed on the ground. One of them reached for the other's hood, but a foot caught the offending party directly in the chest and he was knocked back onto the ground. He clearly had the wind knocked out of him and he was wheezing for breath. Still, he didn't take his mask off. The other guard stood up and stood over the wheezing body. He reached into his pocket deliberately and looked around as if for the first time aware of his being watched. He dared anyone to challenge him and unlike Goliath, none came forward, there was no David present willing to risk his life for the other guard. The man drew a pistol from his robe and aimed it at the breathless man, who, seeing what was happening, tried to crawl away on hands and knees.

But he did not make it far. The gunshot echoed in the mountains and all in the caravan had to hear the shot innumerable times as the echo bounced off the faces of rock that surrounded them. The man who had shot placed the pistol back within his robe and indicated that he wished to confer with the Prime Minister. Prime Minister Kamali went to his remaining bodyguard, and they stepped away from the rest of the caravan, out of earshot. Kathy and Mark had been desensitized to violence to a certain degree, but neither could hide the shock or fear that was written all over their faces. The caravan waited in silence to see what came of the discussion between the two men. The man who had been shot bled rapidly and his blood started pooling under his body. The ground was too hard to soak up his blood and the slope of the mountain directed it to the base. They all watched in morbid fascination as his blood river formed its own path down.

The two men came back and the Prime Minister was the one to speak.

"We will continue on as planned, on as planned" he said. And nothing more. Everyone seemed to be willing to move along as long as they got to quickly be removed from the sight of the body, and they might have quietly moved on if Kathy hadn't spoken out.

"That's it?" she shouted. The Prime Minister had turned his back and was ready to continue. He was not pleased to turn around again and his face gave it away. He was red and his eyes squinted at Kathy.

"Yes," he said. "That is it."

"What happened?"

The Prime Minister did not respond, but snapped his fingers. Two men came from behind Mark and Kathy and picked her up forcibly. They set her on her horse and stood beside her.

"She'll go," Mark said, pushing his way through to his own horse, next to Kathy's. "Don't worry."

Mark gave a meaningful look to the Prime Minister and he nodded at his men. They backed off and Kathy was able to ride freely.

The caravan continued on with one less member as if nothing had happened at all.

CHAPTER 50:

Gabriel and the professor were in Milan in a hotel room. They had opted to fly into Cyprus under assumed identities as it looked more official.

"I'll look like an idiot," the professor said. "I am an academic."

"No," Gabriel said. "You are a blogger. And a very popular one. The most popular male beauty blogger on the internet."

The professor picked up the bottle of hair dye from the sink of the small kitchenette and stared at it with a frown on his face.

"Do I really have to?"

"Yes," Gabriel said. "You have to."

"But it's blue."

"That's precisely the point."

"Who has blue hair?" the professor said turning to Gabriel, who was still sitting on the edge of one of the beds, watching TV. Gabriel stood up, walked to the professor, and took the bottle out of his hands. He squirted some into his palm and then slapped the top of the professor's head.

"The most popular male beauty blogger on the internet has blue hair. Quit whining."

The professor sighed and walked into the bathroom.

"You could have at least let me wet my hair first. I don't want it to be uneven."

Gabriel could hear the professor from the bedroom area as he wiped his hands with a towel and laughed. His persona was less dramatic... just a lowly book promoter named Charles Kiser who did three minute video book reviews. He looked at the lanyard around his neck that had his false name and a smiling picture of him on it. It was him, but it wasn't. His team had been on a no-sleep three day binger putting together their backstories and making sure they tracked on the internet. It wasn't hard to make identities on the web, but it was hard to make them convincing. And they had to be convincing.

CHAPTER 51:

Mark and Kathy exchanged several meaningful looks. They had both noticed. Things were changing again, and they weren't sure if it was for the better. The Prime Minister was having whispered conversations with his one remaining bodyguard, and the remaining members of the caravan all seemed to be on edge. They had gained a significant amount of elevation and extended conversation was difficult. It was hard enough just continuing to put one foot in front of the other as they continued to go upwards. Mark could no longer fathom exactly where they were going, but he had to assume that the Prime Minister had information he didn't have.

When Kathy was almost gasping for breath and had vomited a number of times from overexertion, they reached a flattened-out valley and the party slowed. They had long since gotten rid of the horses and Kathy leaned against Mark for support. He winced, as he too was in pain, but he let her lean against him. The prime minister was walking down the line back towards them. He was going slowly, talking with his men as he went, patting them on the back or sharing a small joke. When he reached Mark and Kathy he gave them a million watt smile.

"Time," he said. "It is time my friends for our party to shrink for the last time. It is no longer possible to carry this many people. It is to be only the four of us."

"The four of us?" Kathy said in a rather small voice, still remembering the look on the Prime Minister's face the last time she had spoken out.

"Yes," Mark said. "The two of us, the Prime Minister, and his bodyguard."

The Prime Minister smiled again, but this time it was just for Mark, and it was not a smile of happiness, but of understanding. Here was a man who understood.

"Yes," he said. "You, me and my bodyguard. I will give you a few minutes to take a break. Let's say ten. Be ready."

He made his way towards the front of the caravan and Mark thought his swaggering gait looked forced; he too must have been feeling the exertion and was going through great pains ·to hide the fact. Mark turned to Kathy to say something to that effect but saw her collapsed on the ground.

Kathy was passed out. And she was remembering...

* * *

When she was seven her father had taken her for a hike through the Ocmulgee National Monument near where they lived in southern Georgia. There were major earthworks built more than 1,000 years ago by the South Appalachian Mississippian culture with several mounds including a burial mound and defensive trenches. The park was beautiful. It was marshland and Kathy loved the feel of humid heat pushing in around her; it was like a blanket. She also loved the wildlife: snakes, beavers, herons, she loved it all. But most of all, she loved spending time with her father. Unlike Remy, Kathy knew her mother well, and spent very little time with her father. Her parents had divorced when she was only two and because of circumstances she was never privy to, she only got to see her father every other weekend. It seemed tremendously unfair to her, as if she was being punished, like she had caused their divorce and this was her just deserts.

In truth, it wasn't any nastier than a million other twentieth century American divorces. It wasn't amicable, and the court system always favored the mother. It wasn't a fair system, but that's the way it was. After several years had passed, Kathy's mother deeply regretted being so vindictive. She could see the look on her daughter's face when it was time to go see her father. She could see that it had been petty for her to push that her ex only got to see his daughter every other weekend instead of every weekend. There was no logical reason to do so. Roy wasn't a bad father. He was a bad match for Kathy's mother, but that did not make him a bad parent. But by the time her mother realized this many more years of bitterness had passed and she was unable to swallow her pride and lift the restrictions, though she knew it would be better for Kathy.

Being a seven year old, Kathy was very easily tired and the marshland humidity that she loved so much was wearing her out. Her father had her sit down on one of the smaller mounds to take a break. She breathed heavily and looked very concerned when her father handed her a water bottle.

"Are you alright, honey?" he said.

"Is this okay?" she said, looking around. "I mean...to stop here?"

"You mean because this might be a burial mound?"

Young Kathy nodded. Her father smiled at her.

"Well if that's all that's bothering you, don't worry. At this point decomposition has won the battle and we aren't sitting on anything but earth. The only thing keeping the deceased alive are memories and these signs all over the place," he said, making a sweeping gesture. Kathy smiled at him. Her father was a scientist and she hoped to be one too someday. She wasn't one of those children who wanted to hear that the sky was blue because it was God's favorite color. She appreciated the scientific answers. In fact, she recognized them for what they were: far more interesting than any answer a human imagination could come up with.

* * *

Kathy awoke to Mark shaking her. "Nothing but earth," she mumbled. "No bodies."

The Prime Minister and his bodyguard were standing nearby, and as she came to she saw them staring down at her. Mark wiped her face with a wet cloth. She was able to sit up and saw that the rest of the caravan had already left. They were alone.

"Shall we continue?" The Prime Minister said flippantly, as if Kathy had not just been unconscious for quite a while. Kathy looked into his eyes and could see that he was not joking.

She stood up shakily, but with determination.

CHAPTER 52:

Remy found himself in southern, Greek-controlled Cyprus without any idea as to how to continue onwards. He had been, up until that point, motivated by a sense of purpose that was both vague and powerful. He knew that he had to get to Cyprus, but he didn't know exactly why. He had been dragged into this whole situation by an old friend that he hadn't seen in years, and he had no logical reason to still be involved. But he was. And he was now in Cyprus, walking down the streets of Tsakistra, sipping a long-since cold triple espresso and wincing at the bitterness. He needed something to fall out of the sky and onto his head...to tell him what to do. Little did he know that nearly that precise thing was going to happen.

* * *

Now that they had successfully gotten into Northern Cyprus, the professor very much wished that his hair-dye had been of a more temporary kind. It had served its purpose. They had been waved through customs, and had even acquiesced to a few autograph requests by some people who only had a vague sense that these were people whose autograph should be had. The professor was unaware that about half of these people were plants by Gabriel Mizrahi. The others were merely sheep.

The professor followed Gabriel wherever he went, because the man genuinely seemed to have a plan. They were headed to an outdoor store, one of those giant warehouse type stores. It reminded him of the box stores he used to grocery shop at with his wife.

"Claude," she would say. "Should we get the one gallon or the two gallon bottle of ranch?" and the professor would burst out laughing. His greatest problem was that he never wanted the American dream that his wife wanted. He never wanted to be the guy that bought his ranch and olive oil in gallon quantities. He wanted his wife, but not her ideals. It was a more common dilemma than he knew. So, shopping with her at the price marts of the world inevitably caused him existential grief.

"I don't know," he would say. "Exactly how much would you like to help our corporate overlords?"

She would be exasperated as always and stare at him. On her good days she would smile and make the decision on her own. But as their relationship went on, she had less good days, and she would be genuinely frustrated in his inability to come up with a better answer than that.

"I'm a democrat, Claude," she'd say on such days. "But that doesn't mean I can't buy a gallon of ranch if I want to."

And the conversation would hit an inevitable spiral that would lead to one of their many marriage-ending knockdown dragged out fights that each of them would regret for the rest of their lives.

He tried his hardest to push these memories out of his head as he followed the unusually quick stride of Gabriel Mizrahi through the store.

"How are your legs?" Gabriel asked over his shoulder, pushing a rack of t-shirts out of his way as he spoke.

"They have feet attached," the professor replied.

"I hope you're better at hiking than making jokes," Gabriel said. "We're going to have to move very quickly."

The professor was confused, as Gabriel had not yet taken the opportunity to explain the theory behind the Prime Minister's hike into the mountains with Mark and Kathy. But at this point, the professor was used to being left in the dark, and he rolled with it. He allowed Gabriel to lead him around the store and pick out a variety of hiking items: backpacks for both of them. A camping stove, rain gear; shoes with metal spikes in them - the whole shebang. What the professor did not see Gabriel buying, but which he was equally stocking up on, were guns. He would find that out soon enough.

CHAPTER 53:

    Mark had been working for the United States government for two years before Kathy started working at the Pentagon. After Kathy had joined the team, he had a hard time pinning down any one event that had happened in those two years. They were a somewhat sludgy blur. It was as if all of the single moments that accumulated to make up those years of government service before the arrival of Kathy lacked any point of reference to give them meaning. After Kathy arrived, Mark's memories became neatly categorized.

    He had been turned down by the Egyptian government to search for a new pharaonic tomb on Kathy's seventh day. It was also the first day that he had had a conversation with Kathy that lasted more than six words. Kathy had been ten minutes late to work on Mark's thirtieth birthday. She didn't know it was his birthday, and neither did anyone else in the office. Mark had no specific memory of any of his birthdays between twenty five and thirty. He had discovered a harsh truth before the coming of Kathy: after college and in the real world, birthdays don't have an inherently exciting meaning. They are simply days. But after Kathy arrived, that ceased to be true for Mark. He found that every moment of his dull government job had become categorized in his brain. It would take him a little longer to realize what this meant, but he was without a doubt, hopelessly in love with his new co-worker.

    Flashes of this went through Mark's mind as Kathy leaned hard on him during their hike. In an ideal situation she would have made camp. At the very least, she should have been allowed to rest for a while. But the Prime Minister was not feeling very generous. The Prime Minister had changed drastically from the peppy, vibrant man who had greeted them in his dining room. The closer they got to their destination, the deeper into the mountains, and the further away from civilization and consequences, the crueler he seemed to become, detached from reality. It was a slow, but inevitably noticeable process.

    Without any consideration he walked ahead of Mark and Kathy with his bodyguard at his heels. He rarely looked over his shoulder to see if Mark and Kathy were still back there. This went on for two days. In the middle of the third day, Mark stopped and yelled at the Prime Minister.

"Stop!" he said. And he stopped walking. He was essentially carrying Kathy. He sat down and let her flop into his lap. His back was against a boulder and it was hard, but comforting. "We won't go a step further until we talk."

The Prime Minister's bodyguard had murder in his eyes but his boss put a hand up and walked slowly towards Mark and Kathy, carefully navigating slippery pebbles as he made his way back. He sat down on his haunches only a few feet away from Mark and Kathy. Kathy was breathing heavily and had her eyes closed.

"Where are we going?" Mark said. "I don't know where Muhammad is supposed to have hid the grail. That's as far as my theory goes. I need some time to think if I'm to take it any further than that. Do you know something I don't, or are you trying to kill us?"

The Prime Minister was silent for a moment, weighing his words.

"Are you familiar with Fariduddin Attar's great poem, The Conference of the Birds?" he asked. Mark stared blankly at him. He was only vaguely familiar with what he was talking about. "It is... basically the story of birds in search of the Simorgh. You can call the Simorgh the ideal king, a mythical winged creature; you can call it God, or whatever you like. That is what they are looking for. It is a very long poem and it is a very large group of birds who go through a great many ordeals, many of which highlight their individual flaws, weaknesses." The Prime Minister's eyes fluttered oddly over these last few words. His voice was nearly shaking with the excitement of what he was saying. "The Persian language...beautiful language, quite perfect for poetry... is full of opportunity for irony and trickery of language. What the birds realize at the end of their journey is that they are the Simorgh. You see... Simorgh, or si murgh when writing it in two words in Persian, means thirty birds. They are thirty birds. They are exactly what they are looking for."

A great silence greeted his explanation in the mountains. Mark did not know where to begin with how poorly the man was reading the story. Did he see their story as analogous with this one?

"Are you suggesting?" Mark began, "That we are the grail?"

The Prime Minister let out a great belly laugh and his laughs echoed back at the travelers.

"Of course not. I am merely trying to explain my theory to you. We will find the grail if we are not looking. The Prophet hid the grail from those who would seek it, but not those who did not seek it. We are no longer seeking the grail. We are simply travelers wandering in the wilderness."

There was madness in the man's eyes, and Mark wondered what he had gotten himself and the great love of his life into.

CHAPTER 54:

As he was walking down the street, his espresso discarded into a bin, despondent, Remy was hit on the top of the head by a duffle bag. He was fuzzy for a minute, and looked up. A voice yelled down at him from an open window two stories up.

"Sorry!" it said.

Remy looked up and saw a young man jumping out of the window and landing on a dumpster. He jumped down from the dumpster and flashed a smile at Remy. His skin was the color of almonds; he wore a tunic. He couldn't have been more than sixteen and his green eyes were blinding with enthusiasm for life. As he reached the ground, another face appeared in the window. It was an angry face. It yelled down at him.

"Maan! Get back here! We are not finished!"

Maan picked up his duffle bag from the ground. Remy was still rubbing his head from where it had hit him, when Maan tossed the bag in Remy's hands.

"Thanks for breaking its fall. Valuable stuff in there. Let's go!"

The boy took off down the street, weaving in and out of the crowd, leaving angry groups of people in his wake. Remy looked back at the building and saw the angry man from the window coming out of the door, no more than thirty feet from him. There was murder in his eyes. Remy took off after the boy, trying to keep up. He wasn't as nimble and had to push people out of the way to even keep him in sight. He left a trail of yells and shouts in his wake and mumbled a few half-hearted apologies. After several minutes Remy looked over his shoulder and realized that they weren't being followed anymore and made it as clear as possible by yelling towards the youth he was following. Maan was just on the edge of Remy's vision, but he began to grow larger. He had stopped running and was waiting for him to catch up.

When Remy got to him he was sitting on a barrel outside a factory building. They were on the edge of town. There seemed to be more cats than people roaming around. The young man was smiling his toothy grin at him.

"Impressed you kept up," he said, putting his hands in his lap. "Seeing as I didn't really intend you to."

"Pardon?" Remy said. He realized how tired he was and put his hands on his knees. He took deep, rasping, breaths.

"Open the duffle bag."

Remy took the bag off his shoulder and set it on the ground. He untied the top and saw that it was full of household china and jewelry.

"I don't understand," he said. "You didn't want to steal these things?"

"No I wanted to run away from home. But my mother's husband cared more about the things I stole. So I sorta gave you up as a sacrifice. You were just...there. Sorry. It's nothing personal."

Remy couldn't help but laugh at the cheek of the young man. It was unbelievable. He lifted up the duffle bag and poured the contents of it out into the alley. Maan looked on, confused, but didn't say anything.

"Guess we don't need those. May need the bag though."

"For what?"

"For running away. I'd like to join you."

"What?"

"Do you have any definite plans?"

"Well no."

"Good. How do you feel about Northern Cyprus as a destination?"

CHAPTER 55:

Gabriel did the professor the favor of explaining to him the theory of Muhammad and the grail. They started out on nearly the same trail that the caravan with the prime minister and Kathy and Mark had taken less than a week before. But it was just the two of them. There was no great supporting cast and they did not have horses to ride. They were on foot. Gabriel insisted it was the best way to go about it.

"The traditional way to do this is to ride horses into the foothills and then dismount and go it on foot the rest of the way up," he said. "That leads to heavy legs after a few days of riding. The first few days of hiking are harder than they have to be because your muscles have weakened on the horse. Yes we will be tired when we reach the foothills, but our legs will be strong and we will not lose time."

The professor took his word for it and tried to keep pace. Gabriel was keeping a fanatical pace that the professor found difficult to keep up with, and Gabriel Mizrahi did not seem to even be tiring out. If the professor had been privy to what the prime minister's eyes looked like at that moment, he would have seen the similarities that were there; the crazed confidence and drunken ecstasy of the chase.

"How is it," the professor asked, putting on an extra bit of speed to try and draw even with Gabriel, "That all of these rich and powerful men are obsessed with finding the grail... and they need someone like Mark Lockheed to do it? From what I've seen you guys already know all of Mark's theories and I haven't seen anyone grilling him for new ideas. To be honest with you – I don't think he has any. I think he has his theories but very little evidence. So couldn't this all have been done without him? Why get him involved?"

Gabriel stopped walking. He put both hands on his walking stick he had been carrying. He looked at the professor in the eyes and for a moment there was clarity in them that surpassed any craze of the chase. He took a deep breath and he rubbed his chin.

"There's a dark secret about rich and powerful men, that isn't really a secret at all," Gabriel Mizrahi said, without a hint of irony in his voice. "Behind every very successful man is not a woman, but a mountain of self-doubt. Yes, you are correct. All of this could have been undertaken without your former student. How many hours do you think Reginald and I have spent poring over texts about this? More than Mark Lockheed I can assure you. He has other things to worry about. But the thing that drives all very successful men is the same: the urge for approval. Mark sharing his theories with Reginald, and confirming what Reginald already thought was probably the most exciting moment of his life and he owns half the damn civilized world. It will never be enough without the approval of someone who is tops in the field. And I fear... even that will never be enough." He paused again. "Does that answer your question?"

The professor nodded and they continued on their way, Gabriel making great haste with seemingly no effort, and the professor struggling to keep up, but less in the dark about the whole situation he had gotten involved in.

CHAPTER 56:

Mark and Kathy were finally allowed to rest. They had traveled well into the night. It had been dark for several hours by the time the Prime Minister's raised his hand and indicated that they could stop for the night. As he always did when they stopped, the Prime Minister's bodyguard sat on his backpack away from the rest of them, started a fire and stared at them over the flames, watchful. Mark and Kathy were recuperating. They hadn't lit a fire and it was getting cold. It was on Mark's mind, but he was so tired that he wasn't sure he'd be able to do it. That was when the Prime Minister Kamali came over with some kindling that were already burning.

He hunched down and pulled some newspaper from his pocket which he placed on the ground before he put down the kindling and placed two logs on top of it. He got their fire going and sat down across from them, apparently intent to work on their fire and not talk.

"Thank you," Mark said, after several minutes of silence. The Prime Minister waved it off and shrugged. He sat down and stretched his legs. His guard appeared to be fully down.

"I think," he said quietly. "I think my bodyguard might be scheming against me."

"What makes you think that?" Kathy was exhausted, but not too weak for some cynicism.

"You are a remarkable woman," he said, "to talk to me like that after everything I have put you through. May I tell you a story?" He seemed to be genuinely waiting for a response so Kathy nodded that he could continue.

"When I was a boy I spent a great deal of time in Beirut with my father. He was a businessman you see, a very brilliant one at that. He took me along on his trips for a reason that has only become clear to me in recent days." A saddened look appeared in the Prime Minister's eyes. He looked pained, but kept his stoic face. "My father was not... was not a very loving man. He seemed to me only capable of expressing himself negatively. When I did something good he would grunt and not look up from his paperwork and his calculator with the thin roll of white paper. But if I did something he didn't like he didn't hesitate to reach for his belt. But I went with him on the business trips. I went partially because I believed that he would be disappointed if I didn't. But I cannot deny that I also went because I was hoping that on those trips he would find a way to show me some positive feelings towards me. What I didn't understand then was that the trips had been his way to do so. Including me in the trip was his way of showing affection. A child has no place on a business trip, no place. But he would bring me along and was no doubt frustrated that I didn't seem pleased by it. Interesting thing this interhuman communication, isn't it? Doesn't work very well sometimes."

The Prime Minister stopped for a moment to chuckle ruefully and stoke the fire.

He continued with a sigh. "There was one particular day on one of these trips when we were in the hotel. He had gone down to the lobby to get a soda when the attack happened. What exactly happened is beyond me at this point. All I really remember is hitting the ground and being on my back, suddenly looking at a sky that was falling down around me. The ceiling was gone and little pieces of paper were trickling down from what had once been the rest of the building. One of them fell directly on the tip of my nose and I picked it from my face and read it. Do you know what it said?"

Mark and Kathy were utterly silent.

"The Grail Society: Cleansing has begun. A fringe group of course. Radical Christians bent on eradicating Muslims. I had nearly succeeded in pushing the image of the grail out of my mind Mr. Lockheed, nearly succeeded. I have become a very successful man. A man that I think my father would have been proud of. But then you published a paper, published a paper. You told the world that the grail, this talismanic object that ended my innocence was in my country, my domain that I have worked so hard to control. And then the floodgates opened and the grail seekers were crawling all over me. Tell me, Mr. Lockheed, do you think I want to help these people? Do you think I appreciate their reverence for such an object? You don't need to answer. I just want you to understand, Mark Lockheed. I just want you to understand what we are doing here. If my bodyguard kills me, now you know who I am as a man."

Before Mark and Kathy could ask any questions, the Prime Minister stood up and walked away quickly. His hands went up to his face as he turned around.

Mark and Kathy sat in a stunned silence for a long time.

CHAPTER 57:

"I've heard bad things about the tunnels," Remy said to Maan, but Maan shook his head and smiled.

"You worry too much, Remy. Way too much. Yes, some of the tunnels are patrolled, but not this one. Trust me."

"Do you have any compelling reasons for me to do so?"

Again the young man showed his toothy smile.

"None whatsoever."

It had alarmed Remy how quickly his young companion had agreed to his plan, and his reasoning hadn't been very compelling either. "I've got nothing else to do," Maan had said. "So I might as well." And he had said it all with that annoyingly infectious smile on his face. He was the type of kid that could be found across cultures: the unflappably confident, but charming adolescent.

Maan felt that he had the world figured out, and Remy envied him for his confidence. He remembered when the world made sense like that. He remembered believing that he had everything in front of him. He didn't know if he liked Maan because he was a likeable kid, or because he made him feel young again. Remy had been searching for a reason why he had chosen to come to Cyprus, to continue this journey that he had no business being a part of. He thought that maybe he had found it. Maybe his reason had literally fallen onto his head.

This reason that had fallen on top of his head now had him riding a rickety, rusted bicycle towards the Northern Cyprus border. They had entered no-man's land, the United Nations Buffer Zone, the demilitarized zone between the two regions and they were lone specks kicking up dust with their balding tires. Remy struggled to keep up with the young man, though he hadn't had a cigarette in days – he simply had forgotten to smoke. He'd been too busy and worried. But nonetheless, Maan was a blur on his bicycle.

"Slow down!" Remy yelled, and the young man slowed, pumping his handbrake. Remy caught up with Maan and they pedaled at a steady pace.

"They're way ahead of us," Maan said casually.

"I thought you were only worried about running away from home?"

"Well who wouldn't be interested in the story you told me? If even half of it is true, I'd like to catch up."

Remy was amazed at the young man's tenacity. He had told him the entire truth and that truth had included a fair amount of bloodshed, but there was no fear in the boy's eyes. He legitimately wanted to be part of the adventure. Remy wondered if he was making a mistake, bringing this innocent teenager into danger, but he wasn't sure if he had much of a choice. He didn't know how to get across the border, and Maan purportedly did.

"How far do you think we are from this supposed tunnel?" Remy asked.

"First of all, it isn't supposed. It's there, and it will get us across. But not too far now. No more than a mile."

"And how do you know it's there?"

"Did you really think this was my first time running away from home?"

All Remy could do was shake his head in disbelief. What kind of kid ran away from home to the hostile nation next door? Maan made his own childhood issues seem far away and inconsequential.

"Now let's pick up the pace again," the boy said, pumping his legs hard and kicking up a cloud of dust into Remy's face. Remy watched as he sped away and he began to pump his own legs harder too. This was the path that he had chosen, and much like several other men in the region at that exact moment, he was hoping that his father would be proud.

CHAPTER 58:

They were nearly out of the foothills and into the mountains proper when it happened. Gabriel was the one to notice it first. He stopped walking and the professor nearly walked into the back of his pack. Gabriel shushed him and got down on his hands and knees. He put his ear to the ground like a Native American tracker, or at least that was the image that came to the professor's mind. Gabriel looked panicked and sat his backpack on the ground. He put his ear to the ground again and made a fist with his right hand. He put his left palm to the ground and his fist on top of the palm and left it there. He stood up as quickly as he had stopped and slung his backpack back onto his back.

"We need to move quickly."

"Why?" the professor said, lengthening his stride to keep up with the Israeli.

"We need some cover and these little pea-sized rocks aren't going to hide our fat asses well enough."

The professor was confused, but Gabriel stopped, just for a moment, to make a point. He put his hands on the professor's shoulders.

"Someone is coming," he said, and turned back around, and quickened his pace.

The professor followed wordlessly, trying to ignore the aching in his feet and legs and back: his entire body. Gabriel never seemed to tire and never seemed to have a problem with quickening his pace even further. It was always onwards and upwards. The professor didn't understand because he wasn't fueled with the same passion as Gabriel Mizrahi, or Prime Minister Kamali, or Reginald Astair. He didn't have what they had, and had he been able to recognize the distinction, he'd have been grateful.

They reached an area of the mountains they could use to hide just in time, and thoroughly exhausted. There was a rocky outcropping with shrubs growing thickly clumped together. This was where Gabriel and the professor crouched down low, their packs slung to the ground in order not to stick up and get them seen, and waited for what was coming. It did not take long for them to be able to hear voices and hooves. There was a large group of men coming their way and thankfully they seemed unaware of two other travelers who were nearer than they could have imagined. The professor clamped his own palm over his mouth involuntarily when he saw the sheer number of people that were filing by them. He lost count of horses' hooves and hooded riders and soldiers with guns. It seemed to be some kind of military unit coming out of the mountains. He looked over at Gabriel, flat on his stomach next to him, and his eyes said it all: they were on the right trail, and they were gaining ground. It felt like an eternity, but in reality it took the Prime Minister's discarded caravan about 10 minutes to pass them and for the two men to finally allow themselves to breathe freely again. Gabriel was just about to stand up when a rough hand grabbed him by the collar and hoisted him up. Another hand found the professor and dragged him up similarly.

"You do have sharp eyes, Tariq," a gravelly voice said.

The professor and Gabriel Mizrahi found themselves face to face with two men who appeared to be soldiers. They had automatic rifles strapped to their backs and wore heavy boots that must have been uncomfortable to hike in. They wore red berets, both of with were covered with dust.

"What have we here?" the man apparently called Tariq said. "Looks to me like two criminals. Probably trying to assassinate the Prime Minister."

"That's most likely," the other man said.

"What should we do about this?"

"Good question."

The professor gulped and Gabriel Mizrahi regulated his breathing. He had come too far to let two Cypriot Soldiers ruin his quest. Much too far.

CHAPTER 59:

Mark Lockheed did not believe in God, which meant that he did not believe in divine intervention, but that did not mean he didn't believe in extraordinary circumstances. If he had learned anything in the whirlwind that had been his recent life, it was that he could only be prepared for the unexpected. And the unexpected was exactly what he, Kathy, Prime Minister Kamali, and his bodyguard got.

It happened during a time of profound silence. Much of the trip Kathy and Mark were chatting or the Prime Minister would monologue out loud to whoever was listening. Now that everything was out in the open, there was little to do but wander ever onwards and talk along the way. The bodyguard in the hood was the only one who never spoke. But when it happened no one was speaking.

It was later in the day, nearly dusk.. It was at dusk that they had stopped talking altogether. Kathy and Mark's sweaty hands were entwined and the Prime Minister walked with a slight hitch from a rock in his shoe. They had been trekking all day with little rest and no one felt like talking anymore.

Kathy was the first to notice that something was amiss. She let go of Mark's hand and he turned to make sure she was okay.

"Something wrong?" He said.

"I think so," she said, but Mark clearly wasn't getting her meaning. He had actually been irritating her the last few days. She had recovered and managed to keep up the pace, yet he was treating her like a child. He was concerned about her health when he should have been worried about more important things. But all things considered, she had to admit that his being concerned about her was sweet, if a bit unfamiliar and thus annoying.

"Are you not feeling okay?"

"No it's not that, be quiet."

She sounded harsher than she wanted to, but Mark shut up at the note of urgency in her voice. The Prime Minister and his bodyguard kept walking. They didn't hear the muttered conversation going on behind them.

That was when a pebble hit Mark on the head.

"Ow," he said, rubbing the spot on his head. Then another, larger rock fell just by hit foot. And then the sound of rumbling was unmistakable.

"Go, go, go!" Kathy shouted and they stumbled back the way they had come from. There was a landslide going down and if they didn't get away quickly they were going to be trapped underneath a mountain of rubble at the very best, and at worst, dead. They scrambled, not looking back, falling over themselves, scraping their hands and faces, doing anything to move away from the falling rock, coming down the mountain.

When the terror was over Mark and Kathy got to their feet and looked around them. They were each bleeding. Mark's face was scraped up and smeared with dirt, but other than a few bruises and scrapes he was fine. Kathy had sprained her ankle and had scraped up her forearms and elbows, but all in all they were incredibly lucky. They looked around but could see very little in the cloud of that was still lingering in the air. They breathed heavily and savored the fact they were still breathing at all.

When the Prime Minister and his bodyguard reappeared, it was like a movie scene. They emerged from the cloud of dust, appearing as if out of nowhere, and seemingly in slow motion. The bodyguard's black cloak had been turned nearly entirely gray from rock dust and Prime Minister Kamali had suffered a broken nose; it was turned dramatically to the right, and Kamali tried to stop the bleeding with a handkerchief. Mark and Kathy didn't know whether or not to be happy that their traveling companions had survived the landslide as well.

The four of them sat down on the ground, up against their backpacks, and shared a silence, much as they had just before the incident had occurred. It is often the case in the human condition, that the things that are the most affecting are also the most averse to being described accurately in words. They were experiencing it firsthand.

CHAPTER 60:

It didn't look like the entrance to a tunnel to Remy. It just looked like a tree that didn't belong. It was a tree that stood alone, and there was a bench under it. There was an inscription on the bench and Remy asked if Maan knew what it said.

"You know I'm Indian, right? Aren't you French? Not American? Can't you tell the difference between Arabs and Indians? I can't believe it!"

"Sorry, I was just really curious and…"

"I'm messing with you. I do speak Arabic. Relax Remy."

"So what does it say then?"

"It doesn't translate perfectly, but if I had to put it into words, I would say that it says to spend some time in contemplation. It is an invitation more or less."

"Well then why don't we?" Remy said, taking a seat on the bench.

"It's a ploy old man. It's to distract people. The entrance is behind the tree… on the other side."

"Still," Remy said. "I think I could use a moment of contemplation."

"Are you joking?"

"Not in the slightest."

So the two of them sat down on the bench in the shade of the acacia tree, the teenager begrudgingly, the older man savoring the moment of silent contemplation, just as the plaque suggested he do. What the older man could not possibly have known was that the young man was thinking deeply, despite the fact that he had not wanted to sit down on the bench. It did not occur to Remy that perhaps the reason Maan didn't want to sit and contemplate, and the reason that he had been so willing to run away from home was that he was unable to sit and contemplate or that he simply didn't want to because he was afraid of what he might find if he did.

Maan was thinking about Akilah. He had not, as he had led his companion to believe, left home simply because his stepfather wasn't a good father to him. That had been the case for a long time and he had been perfectly content to stay at home. Akilah was the reason he felt the need to finally leave home. It had happened the night before he literally fell from the sky and into Remy's life.

Akilah and Maan had known each other for most of their lives. They had been next door neighbors up until two years before when Akilah's family had moved to the other end of town. It hadn't put a dampener on their relationship. Maan had spent the last several years becoming a very good cyclist (as Remy had discovered) by weaving through traffic in the streets of Tsakistra on his way to visit Akilah. He was self-conscious about the smell of sweat he inevitably had when he reached Akilah's house, but she told him that she found it comforting. Her father owned a clothing shop on the market and as she explained it, "It reminds me of when he would come home when I was little and he would pick me up. He was always sweaty after a long day and there was as certain sweetness to it that may just be the memory, but you have it too."

Ever since she had told him that, he had pumped his legs even harder every trip, trying to make himself as sweaty as possible. Sometimes he even did an extra lap around the block, which she saw from her window and chuckled about to herself. Akilah's parents were technically Muslims, but they were very similar to many American Protestants that were religious only in name. They were generally secular, and had no issues with Maan being friends with their daughter. Akilah's father, Asif, was actually quite fond of Maan. He would often ask him to sit with him in their living room when Maan was on his way out to make his curfew, just for a moment. He would ask Maan what he thought about political issues and maybe a book he was reading and they would have pleasant conversation. Asif was trying to get him to talk about his daughter. He could tell what was happening and he was fine with it, but he didn't want to embarrass the young man. He would let Maan bring it up whenever he was ready.

Maan's parents were very different. Both his mother and his stepfather were Hindu and Khatris. Despite the fact that there were not many Hindus where they lived, much less Khatris, they insisted that he should go abroad to find a wife, a fact they were fond of mentioning nearly every day. Maan tired of hearing this. Much like Mark Lockheed, he had little patience for his parents' religious ideas. He just wanted to live his life, and their religious ideas were getting in the way of that. If he did embrace their religion, then he couldn't be with Akilah, which was all he really wanted.

The day he had met Remy had been the day he had finally owned up to his parents about his plans. He informed them that if he was to categorize himself in any way, it would be as an agnostic, and that he appreciated the Hindu culture, but he did not appreciate how it stifled his ambitions. He told them upfront that he was in love with Akilah, that he intended to ask for her hand in marriage very soon and if they couldn't deal with that he would leave.

"Son," his mother had said, tears running down her face. "You may use my luggage to pack your things."

His final act of defiance had been to steal some of his parents' fine china on his way out, which was admittedly childish, but he was angry. He had intended on going straight to Akilah's house and asking her to elope, but Remy had afforded him the opportunity to hide how scared he was with his new situation. He did not doubt his love for Akilah, but he doubted himself, and his ability to live in the real world, and so he had taken on an adventure that was not his own.

He felt the sweat run down his back as he sat on the bench with the Frenchman he was guiding into Northern Cyprus. He took a deep breath to smell his sweet-tinged musky sweat and thought of Akilah.

Remy woke him from his reverie.

"Shall we?" Remy said.

"Yes," Maan said. "Let's do this."

CHAPTER 61:

Gabriel and the professor were, to put it mildly, in a bit of a pickle. The two men who found them had had an argument about what to do with them, but unlike in the movies, this did not afford Gabriel and the professor and opportunity to escape. The two soldiers were smarter than that. They bound the two men tightly and made them sit up against a large rock while they hashed out their differences. The argument was essentially about whether or not they should deal with the two men themselves or bring them to the rest of the caravan.

"We could try and find the Prime Minister to see what he would want to do with them."

"You're an idiot if you think that's a good idea. He'd kill us before he killed them. You heard him back there. We're to go back, and to wait for his arrival. That's it. He was pretty clear."

"Well if we're going to catch up to the caravan we'll have to hurry I can barely see them now and we're wasting time."

"What if they won't walk?"

All throughout this argument the two captives were having vastly differently experiences. The professor was spending his time in an utter panic, thinking about the best and worst times of his life, regretting his drinking and his split from his wife and his differences in philosophy from his wife and the loss of his university job and his mentoring of a particularly bright student named Mark Lockheed...

In the meantime, Gabriel Mizrahi was carefully freeing himself from his bonds. He was thankful that they had decided to tie their hands behind their backs instead of in front. It was a rookie mistake. Gabriel Mizrahi also knew a technique that the professor didn't. He knew, from his time with the Mossad, that whenever being bound, to breathe in deeply and to clench his fists very tightly. When he did this, the veins in his wrists bulged and his muscles tightened, so that it may have seemed like they were tying him securely, but when he ceased flexing and let out his breath he had a little bit of wiggle room. It wasn't much, but it was enough, and the argument between the two soldiers was buying him some time. He had enough wiggle room to locate a small rock behind him and go to work on his bonds.

He worked the rock against the military grade rope and was nearly done when the argument between the two soldiers came to its inevitable conclusion. They were to be lead back to the caravan. He wasn't entirely done with breaking his bonds but he'd have to do his best. They stood up as ordered and after doing so Gabriel Mizrahi (after muttering a short prayer) used his shoulders to force his arms apart with as much force as he could generate in order to break what was left of his bonds. He succeeded in doing two things: breaking his bonds, and dislocating his left shoulder. It was lucky for both Gabriel and the professor and Gabriel that it was his left shoulder and not his right. If it had been his other shoulder, they likely would have died there in the mountains. While his left arm hung limply and painfully, Gabriel swung his right arm at the first bewildered soldier and connected with his jaw. The other soldier reached for his gun on his shoulder but before he could get it, Gabriel rammed his knee in his groin. The soldier howled in pain and fell to the ground where the professor proceeded to kick him in the chest mercilessly. It was no time to be squeamish.

Gabriel leaped on the soldier he had punched and pinned him to the ground. The element of surprise served him well. He brought the soldier's gun, which was still strapped to his back, up against the man's neck. He pushed down on the stock of the rifle as hard as he could until he heard a distinctly unsettling crack, and the man ceased to struggle. He got up just in time, as the professor could no longer keep the other man down. He took the soldier's gun he had killed, took careful aim, and blitzed all of their eardrums, but ending the life of the other soldier. The professor was covered in blood, but none the worse for the wear. Gabriel retrieved a knife from one of the dead soldiers and cut the professor's bonds. While he went about picking up things from the soldiers that could be useful for them, the professor stood motionlessly.

"We have to get going," Gabriel said. "We made a lot of noise. More will come. This isn't the time to grieve."

"Right," the professor said. "You're right", and helped Gabriel to reset his shoulder.

They each took a military knife, and Gabriel took one of the HK416 assault rifles the men had been carrying, but the professor could not be persuaded to take one of the carbines. They also took the isotonic beverage powder and MREs from the soldier's backpacks as their own supply was running low.

They continued into the mountains, a little more jaded, but knowing that they were on the right track.

CHAPTER 62:

The mood was somber enough before the bodyguard spoke. They had barely survived a landslide and hearing him speak did nothing for anyone's fragile mood. His voice was strained and gravelly and he sounded like a Brit doing a bad American accent, but his words were even more disconcerting than his voice.

"I heard gunshots," he said. The Prime Minister groaned and gingerly touched his nose. Mark had straightened it for him at his request, but it had not been without a significant amount of pain.

Kathy leaned forward over her knees and looked at the man who had still not taken off his face cover, and she couldn't fathom why.

"I didn't hear anything," she said. "Did you, Mark?"

Mark shook his head.

"Not now," the gravelly voice said. "Before the landslide. I'm sure of it. Must have set it off. Loud noises can do that."

"Lucky we were still in the foothills when you shot your gun off then, aren't we?" Kathy said, never one to hold back. The bodyguard ignored her comment.

"There must be someone following us," he said without any tone of surprise.

"Could just be some idiot soldiers from the caravan shooting at lizards," the Prime Minister said rather hopefully.

"I think not," the bodyguard said, standing up. "I think we should better be careful from here on out. Look over our shoulders."

"Agreed," Mark said. It was his first contribution to the conversation, but it had the effect of adding weight to the bodyguard's comments. Kathy and the Prime Minister (though he might not have admitted it) put a lot of confidence in the archaeologist.

Even though there were several hours of daylight left, they decided not to continue their hike and to make camp right where they were. They also decided that from now on they would take turns standing guard. The bodyguard volunteered to take the first watch, and Mark said he'd take the night watch.

He was shaken awake with a strange amount of gentleness. The black-cloaked man was on his hunches right next to him.

"If you can't get up I can continue the watch," the man said.

"No, no, I'm fine," Mark said and crawled out from under the blanket that was way too short for him. "I've got it." Mark stood up and stretched and went to claim his spot by the fire that the bodyguard had vacated, but an arm reached out and stopped him. The bodyguard further surprised Mark by slipping a pistol into his hand.

"Better safe than sorry," he said, before silently lying down to sleep for the rest of the night.

Mark spent the night stoking the fire and thinking about things he would have rather not thought about. He could see Kathy and the gentle heave of her breathing from where he sat and in that he found what kept him awake. He could not shake the image of Kathy in mortal danger. The odd thing was that he and Kathy had been in mortal danger quite number of times recently and this was the first time he had really given it much thought. It was the loneliness of being the only one awake in the dark of the night that gave him the opportunity to explore the recesses of his mind that were usually suppressed by more pressing needs.

It was a very long night for Mark. At some point in the night he heard a noise. Exactly what time this occurred is inconsequential. He grabbed the pistol and he heard the noise again. He heard it better this time. It sounded like a bird. It sounded like a bird that had no business being deep in the Kyrenia Mountains. He stood up and followed the sound of the bird.

He stepped quietly in order not to wake up the other members of his party. The bird seemed to be leading him away from his campfire and from Kathy, the Prime Minister, and the hooded bodyguard.

After several minutes of following the sounds he was yet to actually see the bird. He was just about to head back to the camp that he was supposed to be guarding when he finally caught a glimpse of the bird.

CHAPTER 63:

There was a large piece of plywood that had been covered with dirt over on the other side of the acacia tree. Both of the men were a little sad to leave the contemplation bench, each for his own reasons that he kept to himself. They had to kick and claw at the ground for several minutes as the tunnel had been out of use long enough that the soil had literally gotten baked and merged with the grass around the tree and the tree's roots. They dragged the piece of plywood away from the tunnel mouth and looked down into the darkness. Remy pulled a flashlight from his backpack and shone it down the hole. He pulled back as a bat flew by his face and made his heart race. Maan laughed at him and climbed down the ladder. He disappeared into the darkness, leaving Remy feeling foolish and slinging his backpack on his back.

He mumbled to himself as he descended the ladder. He was astonished how long it took it took to get down. The tunnel itself did not begin until he was twenty feet underground. When he reached the bottom his foot was grabbed but he managed to kick out and landed a solid kick squarely on his assailant's chin.

"Fuck!" Maan shouted. "You kicked me in the face!"

Remy fumbled around until he found his flashlight and switched it back on. Maan was crouching in front of him holding his chin, which was bleeding. Thankfully nothing appeared to be broken or dislocated.

"I was only joking," he said. "You need to lighten up."

Remy was genuinely furious. He kicked some dirt from the bottom of the tunnel onto Maan's shoes.

"No, you need to grow up. We're about to illegally enter a country, and you're pulling pranks. Knock it off!"

He adjusted his backpack's straps and started walking down the tunnel, following the thin beam of light that came from his flashlight. He wished that he had taken a better torch. He did not look back but he could hear Maan following behind him, his steps muffled by the shame and embarrassment of being kicked in the face by an old Frenchmen. Remy had to admit to himself that he felt a little guilty about what he had done, but the kid had to learn, and he felt that if he apologized Maan would continue to joke around when he needed to be focused. Maybe Maan wasn't taking it seriously, but Remy certainly was.

CHAPTER 64:

Gabriel and the professor were high in the mountains, gaining on those they pursued. There were many paths into the mountains, as many as grains of sand on a beach, but by fate, divine intervention, or whatever it may be called, they were on the right path. They didn't know it for sure, in any scientific way, but they knew it all the same; they were edging ever closer to a showdown. The professor stopped for a moment, hands on his knees, huffing and puffing.

"Look," he said, pointing from his hips, as he couldn't stand any higher at that moment. "What is that?"

"An optical illusion," Gabriel said, hands on hips, standing up straight. "There's a ravine or a canyon there."

The professor had been pointing to a spot still hundreds of feet above them that looked as if there was a flat shelf through the mountains and out the other side. The light of the sun against the shelves of rock made it appear as if it was solid rock and not a ravine. Gabriel slung the automatic rifle off his shoulder and held it in firing position. He turned off the safety. Before the professor could stop him he had it tucked into his armpit and fired.

They heard the rounds hit something in the general direction of the ravine.

"See," Gabriel said, as if what he had done proved some kind of point.

"You've gotta be more careful," the professor said. "You'll cause a landslide and kill us all."

"There are worse ways to die," Gabriel said. "Come on. We've rested long enough."

CHAPTER 65:

It was a rooster. Mark was being lead into the night by a rooster. It strutted and poked its head forward like any other rooster, but surely this one was a figment of his imagination. It couldn't be a real one. The rooster bobbed its head at Mark and turned around, as if beckoning him to follow. And he found himself following the animal deeper into the night, going upwards, upwards into the mountains. He should have felt afraid, but oddly he didn't. He felt calm and accepting of whatever should come his way. The rooster would repeatedly look back at him, as if making sure that Mark was still following.

Mark couldn't understand why he had not caught up to the bird yet. It had short legs and Mark was walking faster than was comfortable. He should have been breathing heavily, but he wasn't. In fact, he wasn't tired at all, and he wasn't sweating. He was pushed ever onward by determination and a surety of heart that this was the correct path for him to take. He looked down at the ground and saw that the bird was not leaving any marks on the ground; its claws were walking just above the ground, floating above the mortal earth.

The moon shone down more brightly than Mark could remember on their trip into the mountains and he thanked heavens for that. It was a light unto his path and helped him keep the rooster in sight. Keep going the voice inside his head said, and in the moment he did not realize it, but it was the voice of Kathy, who was not with him, but back at camp, fast asleep.

The rooster was far ahead of him but it seemed to him that his eyesight had been extended to make it easier for him to follow the bird. He had to crane his neck to see it, but it was as if the bird was a mere few feet in front of him. This was how he saw the bird stop at a high peak and wait. It was waiting for him to get there. He did not need to rush. The bird was very patient.

Mark climbed and as he got higher he had the urge to strip himself of his clothes. He wasn't hot, or sweating, but he knew that he needed to. His clothes felt as if they were no longer clean, or suitable for wearing. He must take them off. And so he did. He did not stop to take them off, but stripped himself article by article as he walked, and he had never been so graceful. By the time he neared the rooster, he was entirely naked but far from ashamed. He had never felt so natural in his life.

He stopped ten feet before the rooster and waited for something miraculous to happen. He felt that this experience must lead to a miracle. Why else would he feel this way? He tried to walk closer to the animal but he couldn't. Something invisible and unknowable blocked his path. So he stayed a safe distance from the bird and from the edge. The rooster had led him to the edge of a deep gorge. Mark remembered seeing it the day before, but it was far more spectacular up close – much better than the illusion he had seen in broad daylight.
The bird and the man stood face to face without any noise being made for an hour at least. The bird was waiting for something, but Mark did not know what. He was sure that it was worth waiting for, but what it was didn't matter.

After a long time Mark realized what they were waiting for. The moonlight was slowly making its way closer and closer to the edge of the ravine, and Mark knew when it reached the bird, that's when it would happen. He was patient now, as all people who have a destination in mind can be if they are so inclined, and when the time came he was ready for his miracle. But he was disappointed. The bird was indeed waiting for the moonlight, but it did not do what Mark expected.

When the moonlight fell upon the bird, it cried out. Mark was familiar with the idea of the sound of a rooster, from children's books and movies, but the actual force of the sound from a mere ten feet away was an entirely different experience. It crowed a second time and Mark was still in awe of the power of the bird's small body and the sounds it could make. There was a brief pause, but the bird crowed a third time and this time it was as if the bird was looking Mark straight in the eyes as it did it.

When it was finished, it turned its tail feathers to Mark and slowly, purposefully walked off the edge of the cliff. Mark cried out but no noise came from his mouth. He lunged forward but the invisible barrier still remained. All he could do was watch as the bird plummeted to its inevitable death.

Then he was brutally jabbed in the ribs with a rifle butt.

CHAPTER 66:

Maan and Remy had made it across the border and into Lefka without any problems and were speeding in a cab to the northern part of the country. Maan was beatboxing and pounding his fists against the back of the headrest to his own beat; showing his joy at getting out of the tunnel alive. The cab driver was increasingly annoyed as his head was jostled by the youth's enthusiasm, but Remy waved some more bills from the passenger seat and the cab driver gritted his teeth and plastered a forced smile across his face.

"So how do you know we're supposed to go into the mountains?" Maan said, once the cab driver had driven as far as his business conscience would let him.

"The radio broadcast I heard in a coffee shop just before I met you."

"What'd it say?"

"It said that the Prime Minister was on a hunting trip."

"So what?"

"I've tried to contact my friends, an old colleague of mine specifically, and his voicemail on his phone says, 'prime minister.' I'm a scientist; I can put two and two together. The broadcast said he was in the mountains, but if he's up doing anything other than looking for the grail I'm the Easter bunny."

"Nothing is impossible," Maan said, taking a large bite out of an apple. After a short pause in which he had chewed absentmindedly he said, "Akilah's father mentioned that there are some legends of Muhammad wandering in the Kyrenia Mountains."

"Who's Akilah?" Remy asked.

"Just an old friend," Maan said.

From the way that Maan's mood changed and he stared at the ground as they walked for the next ten minutes, Remy could tell that the teenager wasn't being entirely truthful with him, but he didn't push the issue.

"Could take days to get through the foothills," Remy said, somewhat overwhelmed by the expanse of the mountains they found. He had never visualized them in his mind before, but he supposed that if the cup of Christ was hidden somewhere, it should be somewhere grand.

"Yeah if you're an idiot," Maan said. "Or you could just go and take the river to the foot of the mountains."

"Does everyone in the region know that?" Remy said, his interest piqued.

"Well yeah," Maan said. "But it's supposed to lack the spiritual resonance of going through the foothills, or some bullshit like that."

"Maan," Remy said.

"Yes?"

"What would I do without you?"

CHAPTER 67:

Gabriel was a full fifty feet ahead of the professor. He wasn't tired, but he knew the college professor turned thrift art dealer certainly was. He stopped walking and sat down on a rock. He had been contemplating the decision for a few days and it finally seemed like the time to pull the trigger. He needed to stay unemotional when making such a decision. He had to admit, that he had grown to somewhat like the man; he was likeable. He was earnest, which was something that Gabriel had rarely run into in his line of work. He rubbed his knees as he saw the man slowly approaching him. The slow speed of the professor's approach and the haggard look on his face that Gabriel noticed once he got closer confirmed his decision to be the right one to make.

He did not stand up as the professor reached him.

"Are we taking a break?" the professor said. "I know I'm not an Olympic athlete but we took a break an hour ago. I'm good to keep going."

"We need to talk," Gabriel said. "You're slowing me down. It's becoming a problem."

* * *

As he sat on the rock, a full thirty minutes after Gabriel had left, the professor still couldn't believe that it had happened. The Israeli had simply left him there in the mountains to fend for himself. All things considered, he had done it fairly gently. The professor had seen Gabriel do some pretty horrific things, even very recently with the two men from the caravan, though that had been entirely necessary to their survival. He had been gentle and soft spoken, and it only made it worse. That meant he must have been thinking about it for quite a while. It wasn't a spur of the moment decision. Gabriel had clearly been thinking about leaving him for some time. Maybe even before they had been arrested by the soldiers he had been considering it. But the professor had helped with that. Maybe only a little, but he had helped.

He had not been so lost since his divorce and his firing from his job. There was no failing art gallery in the Kyrenia Mountains for him to buy and try to get his life back together. He wanted a drink. He wanted a drink badly. He sat on the rock and basked in the sheer magnitude of his loneliness. Yet he didn't know how close he was to other people. The mountain was teeming with people, both alive and dead.

CHAPTER 68:

Mark awoke to a debilitating pain in his ribs as the Prime Minister's bodyguard stood above him and held his rifle that had clearly just been jabbed much too firmly into Mark's body. Mark winced and blinked and tried to get up. The bodyguard hoisted him up by his shirt and Mark was stunned by the man's strength. When they were face to face, though he could only see the man's eyes, he knew he was scowling.

"Keeping watch does not mean fall asleep," he said without the smallest hint of humor.

Mark was still having a hard time believing that he had been dreaming. Obviously he had been, but it had seemed so real. Despite all of the obvious reasons that it could not have been real, it felt real. He had never had such a lucid dream before and it had certainly seemed more real than the black-hooded bodyguard who stood in front of him now.

It was still the deep of night and Mark wondered what the bodyguard was doing awake.

"Why aren't you asleep?" Mark asked, which was the wrong question.

"Didn't think you were capable of the watch and I was confirmed in that belief."

"Look," Mark said. "I'm fine. I'll be okay from here on out. You can just..."

"Go to sleep," the bodyguard said. "I relieve you of your duty."

Mark did have to admit that he was tired and so he joined Kathy by the other fire. He lowered himself down beside her. In her sleep she had taken his blanket along with hers and he did not try to take it from her. He huddled against her and put his arm over her. He tried to go to sleep, but now that he wanted to, he couldn't.

CHAPTER 69:

Maan was indeed a genius. It only took them six hours to reach the river, and according to the teenager all they had to do was follow the current to get to the base of the mountains.

"Or," he said. "If you prefer, we could keep right on going to the Mediterranean. I hear it's lovely this time of year."

Remy laughed. He was in a great mood. Fortune had shone on him, bringing this teenager into his journey to show him the way. They joked and laughed together as they drew near the river. From a distance they could already see a jetty. They were planning on hiring someone to bring them down the river, as neither of them had any experience manning a boat of any kind, even a canoe or a kayak. They were practically skipping with excitement, but when they reached the jetty they found it empty. They looked around. Jetties are not generally rife with hiding opportunities; they tend to show the truth at face value. The truth was that this one was empty. It was not just empty. It was deserted, and it looked like it had been for some time. There were some planks missing and a few were hanging into the water, waiting to be swept away by time and water.

Remy stepped gingerly onto the jetty, testing it. Decrepit as it was it seemed firm enough, so he walked out further. There were a few boats moored, tied up with cobwebbed ropes. Maan followed him wordlessly, which was difficult for him. He was a young man who generally had words bursting out of him. The silence had a numbing effect. The rush of the river was nothing more than white noise, a complement that seemed only to deepen the silence of the abandoned jetty.

"Guess the Prime Minister has made some changes?" Remy said, breaking the silence, trying to sound positive.

"I heard that Kamali was trying to shut the borders, but I didn't know that meant the Mediterranean too. I mean, what's the point?"

"I get the feeling," Remy said. "That this does not really have anything to do with the conflict with Greece. I think this is more about why we're up here."

Maan was silent and Remy wondered if the young man that was accompanying him had any idea of the magnitude of what they were trying to do. This was not a field trip.

Remy was lost in his own thoughts and was brought back to the present by the sound of a splash. He looked up and saw that Maan had jumped into the river. He was waist deep in the water and was pulling one of the small boats away from the jetty after casually tossing his backpack in it. He waded towards the jetty, pulling himself along by the boat's rope.

"What are you doing?" Remy said.

"We're not planning on sitting here forever and feeling sorry for ourselves are we? This was supposed to be a shortcut. We'll never catch up to all the nutjobs sitting around."

"I'm one of those nutjobs," Remy said.

"I'm sorry," Maan said. "I meant to say we'll never catch up to all those other nutjobs. Honest mistake."

Remy hopped into the boat and felt his first twinge of nervousness as it rocked from his weight.

CHAPTER 70:

Something strange was happening to Gabriel Mizrahi and it wasn't something he could get rid of by shaking his head. The mountain was getting to him. He had heard stories of travelers losing their minds from being alone for too long but it had only been a day. He had wanted to be alone. It was his plan. He could go faster that way. But there was a problem. He wasn't going faster. He thought he was, but when he stopped to take a break he noticed something.

He was sitting on a boulder in a particularly barren area. He noticed that the further up he went, the less plant life there was. It was another form of loneliness. Then he noticed his own footprint. He had been staring at it for days as he looked at the ground as he stepped. He could recognize his own footprint. But this was an older footprint. It was partially rubbed out, but it was there. Gabriel had been here before.

He was going in circles.

That was when he thought he was losing it. Extreme exhaustion had never hit him like that before let alone ever led to hallucinations as it often does to those who are alone in the mountains. No, his mind first went to his own probably insanity. He knew he was losing his mind because he could have sworn that he heard a rooster crowing. There couldn't possibly have been a rooster in the Kyrenia Mountains. He lay down and stared at the sky. The mountain peaks he had yet to reach towered menacingly above him. He was in serious trouble.

* * *

The professor was having a very different experience. He found, that after some time to think about his situation, Gabriel Mizrahi leaving him had been a good thing. Sure, he had been emotional about it first, but Gabriel Mizrahi was a dangerous man, and the whole adventure was far too dangerous. He was better off heading back to civilization. Though his mood was good, his sense of direction was not so great. So he found himself wandering in good spirits yet quite aimlessly. He was going downwards, which was the only direction he was sure was the right one. He decided that he'd figure out the rest once he reached the bottom. He was done with this mountain business. He didn't really want anything to do with it anymore, or so he thought.

As he got further and further down, on top of noticing that going down was every bit as difficult as going up, if not harder, he also noticed a sound. It was a familiar, but altogether surprising sound. It was not a sound he had expected to hear, and he had some pleasant memories associated with it. It reminded him of better days.

When he had first become a full-fledged professor at the University of Chicago, he had loved to take walks around the city. He would wear his blazer with the elbow patches to accentuate his professorial status, and he enjoyed strutting around town. By far his favorite thing to do on these walks was walk along the river. The Des Plaines River was not a pretty river; it never was and it never will be. It was never going to be featured on National Geographic or on the Travel Channel. It was simply a river in a largely industrial city in the Midwest, but Claude the newly-minted professor loved it. What he saw when he looked at it was similar to what devout Hindus see when they look at the Ganges. He didn't see a dirty river full of debris and garbage, but a shimmering surface that hid an endless amount of opportunities just beneath it. He had been a very optimistic man in those days.

And he was feeling that way again as he made his way down the mountain. The Professor heard running water, and while he knew it wasn't his beloved Des Plaines, it filled him with the same kind of joy and he picked up his pace.

CHAPTER 71:

Mark wasn't the only one who had an interesting dream that night. Kathy woke up in a cold sweat. It wasn't a rooster that she had imagined falling into a ravine, but Mark, which is why she couldn't look him in the eyes when she woke up and he was right next to her.

"I need to stretch out my legs," she said.

"Good I'll join you," Mark said, but before he could say any more she put her hand on his shoulder and gently pushed him back onto the sleeping pad where they had been. "I'd like to go alone," she said. "If you don't mind."

Mark was obviously hurt, but he nodded and let Kathy go on her own.

"Don't go too far," The Prime Minister said, blowing on his coffee in his tin mug. Mark couldn't believe that the Prime Minister had brought coffee. In the meantime the bodyguard had come back, but did not say from where.

"Good morning," he said curtly to them both, taking some coffee from the Prime Minister's pot without asking, an act of boldness that Mark wouldn't have attempted in his wildest dreams. And he had been having some wild dreams. It was surprising to Mark that the bodyguard did not bring up what had happened last night. He was quite upset that morning but he said nothing.

"Today," The bodyguard said in his gravelly voice. "Is the day. I can feel it. Something very important. The next twenty-four hours. My intuition tells me."

"Let's hope so," the Prime Minister said, unable to hide his excitement. "I'm ready for this to be over. I've got some dynamite that I'm just dying to put in a very old cup."

The Prime Minister's remark would have been shocking to Mark hadn't he heard him say similar things so many times before. The Prime Minister was a man on a mission that could not be deterred. If Mark had not been so distracted by both Kathy being gone and the comments made by Prime Minister Kamali, he might have noticed how the bodyguard winced at the Prime Minister's words.

"I think we will reach the ravine today," Mark said, pointing at the geological formation that had been so prominently a part of his dream from the previous night.

"Yes," the bodyguard said. "I am certain we will. I have a good feeling about that ravine. Do you know, Mr. Lockheed," he continued. "What is most common in ravines like this one?"

Mark had to admit that he did not.

"Caves, Mr. Lockheed. Ravines like this one are very often replete with caves."

CHAPTER 72:

Maan had taken to river-boating much more than Remy had. A lifelong Parisian, Remy had lived essentially a city-bound life. River-boating had never entered into the equation for him, though he was no longer a young man. He spent much of the trip down the river, vomiting over the side. It was a herky-jerky journey, as they could not locate any oars anywhere near the jetty or in any of the boats. Maan had found a very long pole at the banks and was using it to push the boat down the river. They ping-ponged down the river, using the current and the banks of the narrow waterway to guide their journey.

Maan laughed to the wind and shouted and whooped. At some point he took his tunic off. He wasn't hot, but it seemed like the right thing to do. In his mind, men who were river-bound did not wear shirts. They rode the currents sans shirt and sans fear. At one point he yelled, "I LOVE YOU AKILAH" into the wind and although he was in the process of emptying his stomach into the river, Remy noticed.

Something else that Remy noticed deserved a double-take. He lifted his head for a moment, the urge to vomit shocked out of him. There was a man walking along the river going the opposite direction they were. A man whose gait Remy recognized. He pushed himself up to a sitting position and turned around.

"Maan! Go to shore!" he shouted against the roar that the wind.

"What?" the boy shouted.

"GO TO SHORE!"

"Righto captain!"

Maan took them towards the shore with a punt of the pole and Remy felt his stomach lurch but he didn't take his eyes off the man on the shore, who by now had seen them too. He was waving his arms above his head and jumping up and down like a madman.

The man was the Claude. He had found his old friend, quite by chance.

P.W.Child & Matthew King

CHAPTER 73:

There was a lot of hugging and incomprehensible shouts as the two old friends greeted each other on the shore. Remy had waded to shore, preferring to jump out of the boat before it reached the shore and let Maan moor it in and tie it off on a stump. When Maan was finished doing that he approached the two men, one he knew well at this point, and the other a total stranger.

"This," Remy said. "Is my dear friend Claude."

Maan's face lit up.

"You're the one with the dramatic escape from torture and the middle of the night burial?"

Reminded of that night, Claude and Remy shared an uneasy laugh.

"Yes," Claude said. "That is me."

"What the fuck are you doing here?"

"That," he said. "Is a long story."

"Tell it in the boat," Maan said. "We're in a bit of a hurry."

Claude's story was indeed a long one. Just like Remy he had been through a lot since they parted at the train station back in Paris. When he finished telling it Remy let out a deep breath.

"Well you're going to be disappointed," he said. "Because that's just who we're trying to catch up with and it seems like you've given up on that idea."

"Fuck it," Claude said, making Maan giggle childishly. "Now I'm with friends. I'm game. I've had some time to rest up and reflect."

"And upon some reflection," Maan said. "You've decided to be a crazy sonofabitch again."

"Something like that," Claude replied.

"Well sounds good to me," Remy said.

"ONWARD HO!" Maan shouted, channeling his inner Mark Twain, pushing the boat off with gusto down the river. The wind hit them all full in the face and made them feel alive. Without looking back they were headed for the base of the mountains.

CHAPTER 74:

Kathy tried to shake the image of her dream from her mind. She didn't wander far from camp. Just like everybody else she, too, felt that something was in the air. They all seemed to collectively recognize that this was the day. Something was going to happen and none of them could explain why. She wondered if everyone else had had such vivid dreams. Her dream had been biblical in nature, or at least she was pretty sure it had been. The words echoed in her brain. And they rose up, and thrust him out of the city, and led him unto the brow of the hill whereon their city was built, that they might cast him down headlong. She thought it was from the Bible. The Bible certainly had enough horrible things in it for that to be one of them. She could see the crowd in her mind's eye, lifting Mark high above their heads as if he was a crowd surfing musician. And he got closer and closer to the edge of the cliff. The pushed him and pushed him and he seemed entirely oblivious of his impending doom.

She nearly jumped out of her skin when Mark put a hand on her shoulder from behind her.

"I'm... I'm sorry," he said. "I didn't mean to scare you. But we need to get going."

"We do," she said, surprising herself, clapping a hand to her mouth.

"Yeah," Mark said. "I understand the feeling. I felt it too. We do need to get going. I don't know how I know that, or you do, but everyone seems to be feeling it. There's a palpable urgency in the air up here."

"Let's go then," she said, and took his hand. She carefully intertwined their fingers and squeezed his hand tightly. "Let's go."

The beginning of the end had begun. And everyone knew it.

CHAPTER 75:

Gabriel Mizrahi thought that he was in Israel. He stumbled around, screaming to the mountains about Gaza and the in his opinion pompous idiot Netanyahu. He couldn't believe that no one was listening to him. He had something very important to say but...he just couldn't exactly remember what that was.

A car bomb went off and he ducked for cover behind a large boulder. He scraped his forehead on the boulder and blood gushed out of the wound and into his hands as he clapped them to his head. Night time was coming very early. It was getting dark.

When he woke again, he could hear them: the rebels. They wouldn't take him by surprise. No, no. He would be ready. He was surprised to find that he was carrying an assault rifle. He didn't remember where it had come from or why he had it, but he thanked his lucky stars that he had it. He made sure that it was loaded and he waited patiently. The car bomb had tossed him behind a gigantic boulder and he was well covered. They would never see him. They wouldn't be ready. But he was. They wouldn't take his country in the dead of night. It was still his country and he would die to protect it.

He regulated his breathing as they came closer.

CHAPTER 76:

Claude, Remy, and Maan had made it successfully around the foothills and were at the foot of the mountains. They were wasting no time and had a pep in their step. As they had only just arrived in the mountains, they could not recognize their urgency as the others, who were deeper into the mountain could. But it was an overbearing urgency all the same, one that did not come from them, but from some ineffable force beyond recognition.

.They didn't stop to eat or drink, but unzipped their packs as they went and popped snacks into their mouth or drank some water as they trotted along. They couldn't say exactly why they had to keep going at such a rapid pace, but they all knew they had to. Perhaps if they hadn't been urged on at such a pace they would have noticed that something was wrong. Maybe they would have taken the time to see that the path in front of them looked disheveled, as if a man, hallucinating from exhaustion had stumbled along it and bashed his head on the rock.

They would have noticed that the birds had stopped flying overhead, and that there was no breeze in this little rocky outcropping. They saw no lizards scurrying across the path that they had gotten so used to and that Claude had taken to giving names to pass the time. His favorite had been one with an odd orange discoloration on its head that he had named "Carrot Top."

It would have even been possible that they would have noticed the drops of blood on the ground and the smeared handprint on the boulder soon enough to make a move, to turn back, to change their course enough to avoid the sick man behind the boulder, taking the safety off of the assault rifle that he had taken from the dead body of a soldier from Northern Cyprus.

"Do you ever wonder," Remy said, taking a bite of a granola bar from his backpack. "What a search like this could be like if the academic community took it seriously? If we had the funding that Richardson and his group of idiots studying the Mayans had?"

"Ha," Claude said, looking down at his feet as the lizard with the prominent chin he had called Jay Leno crawled over the tips of his shoes. "We sure as hell wouldn't have to deal with this cloak and dagger shit. It would be much more like university work, or like what Kathy and Mark do. This is, after all, what most people think archaeology is like, not the boring paperwork and the schmoozing to foreign governments to be allowed to dig."

"Thanks Hollywood," Remy said, chuckling and Claude laughed along with him. The easy flow of the conversation was part of their problem. They had allowed themselves to let their guard down in a way that they hadn't done in quite some time. Perhaps with Maan this was to be expected, he was young and had been a part of the fellowship for the shortest amount of time. He should be forgiven for not understanding how dangerous it was to let one's guard down. But it is inevitably the most innocent who pay the price.

"But Raiders of the lost Ark is one of my all-time favorite movies," Maan said. "I watched it about a dozen times with Akilah. We have this movie theater in Tsakistra that always plays old movies. Akilah's father says they steal them or get them from the black market or something, but I don't care. Those have been the best Sundays of my life."

"But you're a smart kid," Remy said. "So you can understand that Harrison Ford is not an archaeologist and that the movie isn't an accurate depiction of our field of study."

"Yeah," Claude said. "It's not generally a good rule to rely on the intelligence of movie-goers though."

Maan laughed at the two older men and allowed himself to remember those Sundays with Akilah, holding hands in the dark, air-conditioned movie theater, not regretting for a moment the loss of all his week's spending money, being swept away by the magic of cinema. They couldn't take that away from him. Nobody could. It could be said of Maan, and for this he is fortunate, that his last thoughts on this earth were positive ones, some of his best. Most people can't say that.

"You two could not sound older," he said, turning his head around to look at the two archaeologists, and he could tell from the looks on their faces that something was very wrong. They weren't looking at him. They were looking over his shoulder as Gabriel Mizrahi emerged from behind the boulder, gun pointed directly at Maan.

CHAPTER 77:

They were very close to the ravine now. Mark and Kathy simultaneously wondered, oblivious to the other, how, if they actually did find the grail, they were to protect it from destruction, and why they were so sure that this ravine held the answers they were looking for.

"Stop," the Prime Minister said. The group stopped and all eyes were on him. "It's time," he said, nodding to his bodyguard. He turned to Kathy and Mark. "I do hope you will be amenable to a few changes in our situation. Minor, of course."

"Why do I get the feeling that we have a different definition of minor?" Kathy spat.

Mark remained calm. He had more or less expected this moment to come. He didn't know when exactly it would come, but it was rather obvious to him that it would. They had explicitly different goals in mind for the journey, and the Prime Minister had more power where they were. He didn't fight it because he knew it was pointless to do so. He had come to a conclusion while they walked, after his dream. In his dream, he had been frustrated by the invisible wall. He was now ready to accept it. He would not attempt to change what he could not. If the grail existed still, then it had survived thousands of years without Mark Lockheed to find and protect it. It was probably better off anyway. If it was meant to survive Prime Minister Kamali's hatred, then it would, with or without Mark Lockheed.

"Bind their hands," the Prime Minister said, and Mark stuck his out willingly. Kathy looked at him pleadingly, begging him with her eyes not to give up so easily. He could not explain so simply with his eyes that this was not giving up. After seeing that Mark was not going to fight it, she too put out her hands and they were both ziptied.

CHAPTER 78:

As he struggled with a clearly changed Gabriel Mizrahi, Claude tried to talk him down. The Israeli had seemed clear-minded enough only a few days before when they had parted ways. After all, he had rationally decided that he would make his way up into the mountains faster if he didn't have Claude around to slow him down. But this man that he was wrestling to the ground was not rational, and Claude wasn't even sure if the old Gabriel Mizrahi was still in there. He snarled like an animal and bit Claude's hand.

Blood streamed from the back of Claude's hand and into the dirt, as Gabriel tried to get out from under him. Claude kicked his leg out and tripped Gabriel up. He managed to grab the assault rifle and point it at Gabriel. He could vaguely hear Remy sobbing behind him, but he didn't have time for that at the moment. Everything he knew about Gabriel Mizrahi flashed through his mind as he trained the gun on him. Gabriel was certainly not a kind man, and he had the blood of many on his hands, but the professor was not a killer and he couldn't pull the trigger.

"Go," he said, gritting his teeth, trying his best not to cry. "Just go."

"Claude," Remy said. "Are you crazy? Shoot him. Shoot him now!"

"No," Claude said. "No. Go on. Get out of here. Don't you get it, Remy? We're looking for something that's supposed to be holy? The man who supposedly drank out of the cup said to love one another as I have loved you. Turn the other cheek. How many have died for this artifact? What would the man it belonged to think about that? I am not a religious man but I can't. I can't, so go. Good riddance, Gabriel."

Gabriel Mizrahi ran away without paying much attention to the path he was running on. His clothes flapped in the breeze as he ran like a rooster with its head cut off.

Remy sobbed as Gabriel ran away. He was hunched over the body of Maan, that innocent teenager he had brought into this adventure so selfishly. He had simply been the first person to drop into his lap who could have helped him. He could have kept looking by himself, kept wandering around Cyprus with no idea what to do. That would have been better probably. At least Maan would still be alive, still watching Hollywood movies with the love of his life.

"He loved that girl," Remy said quietly, sitting down next to the body that would not move ever again. "The girl who he went to the movies with...he loved her. He said so on the boat, when he thought I couldn't hear. He shouted into the wind that he loved her. And now he's gone. For what? An old cup."

"Akilah," Claude said. "Her name is Akilah."

"Yes. That's her name," Remy said. "Akilah."

"He loved you Akilah," Claude shouted. "He loved you!"

Remy joined in and the two of them shouted to the heavens that Maan had loved Akilah. They mourned the fact that there would be no happy end for these young lovers, because a crazed man had put an untimely end to Maan's life.

"Thank you," Remy said quietly, standing up.

"I think," Claude said. "We owe it to him."

"We don't have a shovel," Remy said. "And we're in a hurry."

"What are we in a hurry for?" Claude asked, and Remy was unable to answer.

The two men got down on their hands and knees and began to dig with their hands. The land was rocky and hard but they would dig until their fingers bled. Maan would have a proper burial, and the two men would bury a man together for the second time.

This was where they were when everything went down, and they didn't regret it for a moment.

CHAPTER 79:

The sight of the ravine was undeniably majestic. It was nothing like it had been in Mark's dream. Dreams are personal and the ravine had seemed to have been deeply personal in his dream, a tiny section, just enough space for a rooster to crow three times and then commit suicide. But in reality, it was massive and awe-inspiring. The group had little time to appreciate its majesty as the Prime Minister had them marching along the edge.

"We are looking for a cave," he said, matter-of-factly. "It could be on this side of the ravine or on the other. We may have to check several."

Mark had to hold back a laugh at this. They might have to check several? There could have been hundreds of caves in the Kyrenia Mountains, but the ravine was doing its work on the Prime Minister. The Ravine could get into a man's thoughts and tell him what was real and what wasn't. And it was a liar. Mark had found himself in a less trance-like state once he had decided that he would not bother with fate, would not bother with what he could not control. In doing so, he had unknowingly freed himself form the ravine's spell. But the Prime Minister had done no such thing. He was convinced that they were near and that it was time to do something about it: something drastic.

CHAPTER 80:

From where Claude and Remy were digging with their sore hands the first thing they noticed was one pebble. It came bouncing towards them down the path and came to a rest near Remy's shoe. He picked it up and they both stared at it. The pebble was a different color from all of the rocks and soil around where they stood, and they wondered where it could have come from.

What they did not know was that the pebble had come from way above them, from an explosion near a ravine that would result in death for some.

Unable to explain the phenomena, Remy handed the pebble to Claude, who placed it into his pocket to have another look at it later before they continued digging. They had dug out nearly a foot deep a hole long and wide enough to be the final resting place Maan, the young runaway.

CHAPTER 81:

"You two stay here," the Prime Minister said, his eyes glowing with excitement. He received no complaints from Kathy or Mark. They would remain where they were instructed, near the edge of the ravine.

They had discovered a cave, and the Prime Minister had decided that it was the one. Only someone as deluded as he was could have decided with such a degree of certainty that this must have been the cave, and evidently his bodyguard agreed. They were to go into the cave together and look for the grail of which they were certain that it had to be in there.

The bodyguard paced excitedly before the mouth of the cave, which was little more than four feet tall, as the Prime Minister explained to Mark and Kathy that they were to remain where they were. Mark could see him over the Kamali's shoulder, itching to finally go into the cave.

"When I see you again," the Prime Minister said, strapping a headlamp around his head. "I will be a changed man, and it will be a changed world." He gave them a wry smile. "For the better," he added, and the effect was sinister, but they let him go.

Mark and Kathy watched as the two men, one still hooded, ducked and entered into the cave in the side of the mountain.

"It's insane," Kathy said. Mark simply nodded in affirmation. "What do you think will happen to them?" Kathy asked.

Mark was silent for a long moment, weighing his answer.

"Only God can tell," he said, and Kathy stared at him, shocked at his words. But it was not the time to talk about beliefs. It was time to be more practical.

"You know," she said. "We could leave. They could die in there for all we know. Why not just leave now?"

"It doesn't feel right," Mark said. "There's something wrong with them."

"Yeah," Kathy said. "Fanaticism. You don't want to leave them in there?"

"I don't want to leave them in there," he said.

"So be it then. I won't leave you."

And so they waited. And waited. And several hours later, as dusk was coming on, the two men emerged from the cave again. The Prime Minister hardly seemed to notice they were there, but scrambled to his backpack.

"Too small," he said. "The opening is too small we'll have to make it bigger. Make it bigger. Gotta blow a bigger hole so we can get through. Get to it. It's back there I can tell. Back there I can tell."

He picked up his backpack and brought it to the mouth of the cave. Mark stood up to get a better view of what the Prime Minister was doing. He was pulling something out of his backpack, but he couldn't see exactly what it was until he got a little bit closer. Dynamite. It was dynamite. The Prime Minister was stacking dynamite near the mouth of the cave. Mark couldn't believe it. He really had lost it. This high in the mountains, so close to a drop-off, setting off dynamite was utter lunacy. But that did not stop Kamali. He was connecting the fuses now, walking backwards from the stacked dynamite, closer to the edge where he had instructed Mark and Kathy to stay.

"Out of the way," he said. "Out of the way!" he nearly shrieked at Mark as he shoved him out of the way to lay his fuse.

He had just struck a match to light his fuse when he froze. He was staring at his bodyguard who was hunched over something by the mouth of the cave. Only the back of his black cloak could be seen and it looked like he might be rubbing his hands together.

Then everything happened very quickly.

The Prime Minister dropped the match and it caught the fuse. The fuse shot off towards its target with Mark and Kathy's eyes glued to the sparking rocket, headed to the stacks of dynamite, no more than fifteen feet away. Mark and Kathy stood up and began to run. Their captors gave no mind to them; their minds were elsewhere. Mark and Kathy both started to run and stumbled as their hands were bound, but they did as best they could. Though it was unwise, Mark could not stop himself from looking back, and what he saw would be burned into his memory forever.

The Prime Minister grabbed his bodyguard by the shoulder and spun him around. The bodyguard was clutching a large rock, but the Kamali clearly didn't see it that way. The two men struggled over the rock as if it was something precious. Both men were under the shared delusion that the bodyguard had found the grail. They stumbled and struggled ever closer to the edge, as they clawed at each other's faces and blood was drawn.

As the Prime Minister clawed at his bodyguard's face, the hood the bodyguard was wearing finally came off and his face was laid bare. Mark would never forget the last time he saw Reginald Astair. The two men got ever closer to the edge, but neither seemed to notice. They were both focused only on getting the grail for themselves.

They went over the edge together, each man with his hands firmly clasped to the rock. It was nothing more than a rock, just as the grail would have been nothing more than a cup. The last thing Mark saw before the explosion was the look of utter joy on the two men's faces as they clutched what they had so long looked for, and plummeted to their inevitable death.

That was when the dynamite went off.

CHAPTER 82:

"I'm sorry dad, I'm really sorry," Mark muttered. "I tried. I did. I tried for you."

"He'll be okay," the doctor said, letting her stethoscope drop back around her neck. "He's just dreaming. It doesn't have anything to do with the trauma he sustained. I don't want you to worry."

Kathy was sitting next to Mark's hospital bed. The chair, which was supposed to stay beneath the window, had been pulled up to the very edge of Mark's bed. She had just gotten off the phone a few minutes earlier with the professor. He was back in Paris and was having some meetings with the university. Remy was spearheading the movement to have him reinstated. They thought it was going well, and they sent their best to Mark. "The doctor says he'll be okay," she had told them, but she wasn't quite as confident as the doctor.

She thought about that short time ago when she had asked Mark to drinks nearly every day. He had always turned her down, but something had made her keep asking. Something inside her had known that the adventure was in him. Only, she hadn't known what kind of adventure she had been seeing. She had only been thinking about romance. As it turned out, the universe had something else planned entirely.

Mark's breathing was deep and normal and she sat down in her chair. She pulled a book out of her purse and thumbed the pages, her heart not really in it. It was Zealot: The Life and Times of Jesus of Nazareth by Reza Aslan, a book about the life of Jesus. She couldn't quite bring herself to read it after what had happened.

Their entire trip had seemed on a path of divine destiny. They had escaped death so many times, and Kathy had a hard time believing it had been for no reason. Not for no reason, she reminded herself, looking up at Mark, the breath from his nose fogging the tubes that went up his nasal cavity. It just hadn't turned out as they had planned. But she wondered if that was for the better. What exactly would have happened if it hadn't been so disastrous? What would they be doing right then? Maybe they'd be in jail. Maybe they'd be doing an interview on BBC, or maybe they'd both be dead. If there was anything she'd learned on her trip, it was that men who tended to be obsessed with the grail did not have a long life expectancy.

And yet, she could not bring herself to say it was over. With things like the grail, it was never over, not really. She reached into her pocket and pulled out a pebble. She turned it over and over again in her hand. It looked almost like granite.

CHAPTER 83:

Mark sat across from a man in the impeccable suit. He kept his face placid, unreadable. The older, government lifer tried to read Mark but couldn't do it. He steepled his fingers and put his mouth behind it. He let out a deep breath. He as a pro and he knew how to kill time until someone who was lying would crack. What he didn't know was that Mark Lockheed had changed since he had last stepped foot in the Pentagon. This man hadn't changed, and neither had the government work.

This man, his name Roberts, was one of Mark's superiors at the Pentagon. He was one of the interchangeable suits who decided important matters that he knew very little about. That morning he had received a file with Mark's name on it. Someone else in his office had received one with Kathy's on it. It explained that both of them had "contracted pneumonia" at the exact same time and had not appeared at work for more than a month. Neither of them had notified their superiors in any way because they had been "too incapacitated" to do so.

Roberts did not believe this for a moment, but what he and Mark both knew was that he couldn't prove Mark was lying. Despite the fact that Mark's face was tanned and he obviously had not spent the last month in a hospital bed. In truth, Mark had changed more on the inside than the out, but Roberts didn't know that. He probably imagined that this archaeologist had grown tired of government work and had taken off for Aruba, blowing his savings in the process. He'd seen it happen hundreds of times. He had been working in his own version of "the hole" for nearly forty years, and there had been no shortage of days where he had thought about it.

Mark drummed his fingers on the table. The barista at the counter who was steaming milk looked up at him. Mark smiled at the young girl with the stretched ears and the Tolkien tattoo on her forearm.

"Was there anything else?" Mark said, forcing the man's hand. "I know there's gotta be paperwork in this. Believe me," he said, laughing. "It was the first thing I thought of when I was fully conscious of my surroundings again. That's how I know I'm really a government employee. Know what I mean?"

"Indeed," the man said, clearing his throat. "Just one more thing, Mr. Lockheed. It's about Kathy Rollins. Did you see her during your hiatus?"

"What was that last name?" Mark said, leaning over the table.

* * *

"Hey the Minister is back in town," Gates said. "Interesting that I was out on assignment and got back before you did. How'd that work out?"

Mark simply smiled at his co-worker. Truth be told, he was happy to see Gates again. He was even happy to see "the hole" again. He walked back to the coffee maker and emptied out the old filter. As he was pouring new water into the coffee maker the door to "the hole" opened again. Mark turned around to see Kathy beaming at him and walking by Gates. She walked directly up to him and kissed him on the mouth. Gates was stunned.

"What's on the agenda for today?" Kathy said.

"Paperwork, nothing but paperwork."

"You know what?" Kathy said. "That sounds wonderful."

THE END

The Relic Hunters return in

OPERATION NEXUS ONE

56622243R00119

Made in the USA
Lexington, KY
26 October 2016